IN ARCADIA

Ben Okri has published many books, including *The Famished Road*, which won the Booker Prize in 1991. His work has been translated into 26 languages and has won numerous international prizes including the Commonwealth Writers' Prize for Africa, the *Paris Review* Aga Khan Prize for Fiction, the Chianti Ruffino Antico Fattore International Literary Prize and the Premio Grinzane Cavour Prize.

The recipient of many honorary doctorates, he is a vice-president of the English Centre of International PEN and was presented with the Crystal Award by the World Economic Forum for his outstanding contribution to the Arts and cross-cultural understanding in 1995.

He has been a Fellow Commoner in Creative Arts at Trinity College, Cambridge and is an honorary fellow of Mansfield College, Oxford. A Fellow of the Royal Society of Literature since 1997, he was awarded an OBE in 2001.

He was born in Nigeria, and lives in London.

On *Dangerous Love*

'Okri's masterpiece to date... solid, convincing and classical.'
Sunday Telegraph

'Poetic writing of a very high order... tender, nightmarish, wise and soulful tragedy.' *Daily Telegraph*

'One comes to inhabit it as one reads... A reason for constant celebration.' *Scotland on Sunday*

'One of the world's finest writers... A life-affirming, lyrical book.'
Options

'A tough, ecstatic book.' *Independent on Sunday*

'No other contemporary author captures the ephemeral with as much success. Okri should easily pass the hundred year test.'
The Good Book Guide

'Intelligent and moving.' *Spectator*

'The rippling, translucent style is deliberately pared down to tell a simple, memorable narrative of ambiguous love and disaster.'
Mail on Sunday

On *Astonishing the Gods*

'A modern-day classic.' *Evening Standard*

'Amazing... This is as close as you can get to reliving the experience of a bedtime story.' *Guardian*

'Powerful, sensuous and philosophical.' *European*

'Graceful and enigmatic... Exciting, like a trip into a de Chirico landscape.' *Daily Telegraph*

'A new creation myth... a beautiful book... its mere task to make the impossible possible.' *Scotsman*

'A rare achievement... Fulfills Calvino's prescription for lightness – being like a bird, rather than a feather... an impressive, brave, and often beautiful little book.' *New Statesman*

On *A Way of Being Free*

'Okri imbues these essays with a writer's insight… And he does so in an inimitably sinuous yet abstract style well suited to his theme… oblique, oneiric, rhapsodic, elliptical.' *Independent on Sunday*

'There can be no mistaking Okri's passion and intelligence.'
Sunday Telegraph

'Okri is marvellously enthusiastic at promoting the poetic cause, pouring out his love for creativity in "The Joys of Storytelling" with a passionate reverence.' *Daily Express*

'Thoughtful, concise, cultivated and clear.' *Scotland on Sunday*

'Okri is at once as foreign and as British as Joseph Conrad.'
Daily Telegraph

On *In Arcadia*

'Incantatory beauty. Profound and enchanting.' *The Times*

'A charm and magic that is bright and striking and angry.' *Irish Times*

'Mixing a densely metaphysical approach with a delightfully lyrical style… a truly fascinating work, and a hugely ambitious one too.'
Scotland on Sunday

'The shaman of modern British fiction.' *Independent*

' You cannot fault Okri for confronting the big issues and asking questions of our secular age that few of his contemporaries have the innocence and bravery to attempt.' *The Observer*

'Arresting and evocative.' *Times Literary Supplement*

'Okri has chosen a big and bold subject and a highly original approach to it.' *Herald*

'The journey has inspired writers from Homer to Chaucer onwards… Okri gives it an ultra-modern twist.' *Daily Mail*

'A riddling quest for enlightenment.'
Independent.

BEN OKRI

IN ARCADIA

HEAD
of ZEUS

First published by Weidenfeld & Nicolson in 2002

This paperback edition published in 2014 by Head of Zeus, Ltd

9 7 5 3 1 2 4 6 8

A catalogue record for this book is available from the British Library.

ISBN (PB): 9781784082574
ISBN (E): 9781784081850

Printed in the UK by Clays Ltd, St Ives Plc

Head of Zeus Ltd
Clerkenwell House
45-47 Clerkenwell Green
London EC1R 0HT

WWW.HEADOFZEUS.COM

To You

Introduction to the new edition

The books we least expect from a writer can often be the most revealing.

It can be said that writers are most like themselves when they are most unlike themselves. No writer tries to be unlike themselves, of course, but every now and again an unusual inspiration shows an unexpected aspect of one's spirit.

This novel begins with an angry tone which becomes progressively lighter as some kind of epiphany is reached. It was meant as a journey from despair to liberation. Writing a book changes the ideas you had about it before you began. This book changed as I wrote it.

Sometimes a lived experience gives one the contours of a story. Radically altering the experience, but retaining the form, can yield something surprising. One of the frissons of the *roman à clef* is the speculation it engenders. A man once confronted me at a train station with the mistaken idea that one of the characters in the novel was actually his wife. The truth is that the characters in the novel are entirely fictitious. This elastic perception of character has interesting implications for works of the imagination.

Many of my themes are here in this novel in oblique ways. I wanted to try for something new, in a tone new to me, which had its origins in a short story I wrote about London many years ago.

All the characters think they are on a particular journey, when in fact they are on another, more mysterious, one. That is how it is for all of us, I suspect. The journey alters with the living and the telling.

I wanted to come at something known from an unknown angle, like looking at oneself from the point of view of the stars, telescope inverted. We never write the book we think we are writing. We never read the book we think we are reading. All is changed by the angle, the consciousness, and the rereading.

Little Venice, London
August 2014

In this book I use the outer facts of a real journey as a vehicle for fictional characters.

The characters in this novel, therefore, bear no resemblance whatsoever to any living people or individuals. They are imaginary creations.

The journey is real, but the people are invented.

PART ONE

PART ONE

BOOK ONE

One

In our different ways, we were all on the verge of nervous breakdowns when the message came through. We were to follow inscriptions that would lead to treasures hidden in Arcadia. Of course, it wasn't as simple and straightforward as all that. Things rarely are. They proceed in roundabout ways, as if through a constantly changing labyrinth. The message came obliquely, in broken bits, like shards of rare porcelain.

We were, in our different ways, still hoping for something to turn up and save us from the abyss. Some scrap of luck, a miracle, a piece of good fortune, a new kind of bible that would straighten out the awful miserable mess of our lives.

We were all shipwrecks and derelicts on the ruined shores of the city. All wretches clinging on to sanity's last nerve. We were doomed and hopeless, full of fear and failure, and we were masquerading our failures with a certain amount of public dignity when, out of the blue – out of the dark, more like it – came the summons.

It was an intriguing project, a television film about a place we'd never heard of, a place called Arcadia, a place that's supposed to be loaded with classical allusion, but one we didn't give a damn about. All we wanted was to work again, to be on the road again, away from all the problems, all the failures, all the messed-up relationships. We just wanted to get away from our miserable attempts at propping up falling lives, away from the dehydrating boredom of the daily round in this inferno that we call the modern world. We were just glad of anything, and if it meant going to some place called Arcadia, then so be it. We'd go to the end of the earth with an ill-fated Columbus or Sinbad if we had to. Just getting away and doing something vaguely like real work was enough.

And so we got the summons. It came first from a guy called Malasso, an evil-sounding name if ever there was one. But names don't matter till afterwards. He was supposed to be our contact man. He was supposed to co-ordinate the whole adventure.

There it was. We had a contact man, whom no one had ever seen, or ever heard of before. And yet he was our co-ordinator, and only he knew the routes. The job seemed simple: conduct a few interviews, take a few shots of foreign places, allow a few strangers to travel with us, ask no questions, follow the inscriptions, submit to strange encounters on the way, arrive at Arcadia, film a few goddamn goats and sheep, let the strangers sort out the treasure, keep our nose out of their business, stick to the job, and when the shooting's done, come back home, and get paid.

It sounded simple enough: a straightforward journey, fringed with film glamour, paid hotel bills, good food, free trains, and money at the end of it. What business did we have with the other murky stuff tagging along? They were funding our escape, and escape's what it was all about. When everything is said and done, given the anxiety and stress, the nightmare in which we stewed, escape is what it was all about. We would have escaped from life if we'd had the courage, but we were all cowards, and so we stuck around and wallowed in our own bile.

We had all lost something, and lost it a long time ago, and didn't stand any chance of finding it again. We lost it somewhere before childhood began. Maybe our parents lost it for us, maybe we never had it, but we sure as hell didn't feel that we could ever find it again, not in this world or the next. And so the only thing for us was the journey, the escape, the way out, the fake adventures, the phoney illuminations, the exaggerated and desperate joys. That's why we did it, that and getting paid. But there are some things on earth that one shouldn't see, or get paid for, or witness, or do, or suffer, or discover about oneself. We went too far, beyond the rim of things. And maybe we would have stewed in hell till the end of time, as we deserved, if it hadn't been for two things – that crazy girl who fell in love with one of us, and those damned inscriptions.

Two

But I jump ahead of myself. Always been jumpy that way, can't help it. Never had a reason for serenity. Been jumpy since I popped out of my mother's womb. I guess it's the heat of the world that makes me so nervy. I've been feeling that heat as long as I can remember.

Anyway, I've got to tell you how it happened, how the eight of us got together, got summoned, got deceived, got used, and got put through so much hell just because we were in hell already. I suppose that's the way it always is. Contrary to the law of magnetism, like attracts like. Maybe unlike attracts unlike too; and maybe, even worse, even truer, the unlikely attracts the unlikely.

How did it all start, that's what I keep asking myself? As far as I can make out it began with someone having the crankiest notion, in our cynical times, that we should make a film about a journey to Arcadia, to a place of rural tranquillity, a sort of Garden of Eden, our lost universal childhood.

Why anyone would want to make a barmy film like that is beyond me. Who cares if we have lost our childhood, or whether we have lost our way? Who gives a chicken's fart about the Garden of Eden and rural tranquillity and improbable things like that? No one thinks about that stuff any more. No one believes in it. All we care about is the next pay packet, the next meal, the next gratification, the next party, the next football match, the next sensation.

But there you have it. Folks are going out of their minds,

falling apart, hanging out in the fag end of the long centuries. We've lost all our beliefs, our innocence, we've forgotten that we were ever children, we don't care any more, we loathe ourselves, and resent our neighbours, we're eaten up with jealousy and malice, gorged with sin, choking with rage, gasping with failure, and then some feeble-brained idealist has to go and cook up this notion of a film journey to Arcadia.

They think they can sell the blasted notion to television. Someone's paying for it, so why should I care? That's the way the world is these days. We all do things we don't believe in, and we do them passably well. In fact, when you come to think of it, how can you do something if you believe in it – especially in these times when a fine hypocrisy is absolutely essential to success? The less you believe in something the better you can do it seems to me the perfect axiom of the times in which we live.

That's the way it is. If you believe in something your very belief renders you unqualified to do it. Your earnestness will come across. Your passion will show. Your enthusiasm will make everyone nervous. And your naïveté will irritate. Which means that you will become suspect. Which means that you will be prone to disillusionment. Which means that you will not be able to sustain your belief in the face of all the piranha fish which nibble away at your idea and your faith, till only the skeleton of your dream is left. Which means that you have to become a fanatic, or a fool, a joke, an embarrassment. The world – which is to say the powers that be – would listen to your ardent ideas with a stiff smile on its face, then put up impossible obstacles, watch you finally give up your cherished idea, having mangled it beyond recognition, and after you slope away in profound discouragement it will take up your idea, dust it down, give it a new spin, and hand it over to someone who doesn't believe in it at all.

That's the world. Take it from me. I've been chewed over, had my ideas stolen and changed, had my best dreams mangled and mashed up, I've had power work me over and twist me round. I've supped most of my life on the bitter dregs of disillusionment, and now I'm a child of my times. My heart is ash. My feelings are frozen. My eyes are dead. My thoughts are cold. Nothing stirs in me. Nothing surprises me. I expect the worst. Human beings stink. That's a fact. And so when some idealist comes along with some sentimental notion about finding ourselves again and tranquillity I sort of get murderous. They make me edgy; they get on my nerves. To my mind no one's got the right to be happy, or to smile about anything. And I can't stand those who go about as if everything was just fine, as if life was a holiday, a dream, a theme park, when, to all intelligent people who have lived and experienced the real stuff of living, when to those of us cursed with true sensibility, betrayed every day by the injustices of the world, life is clearly akin to a long spell in prison, a long illness with no remission, a nightmare, a hellhole, a freak show, a ship of hypocrites, a house of opportunists, a landscape of fools.

But that's all by the wayside now. The main thing is that here is a job. It makes me jittery but, being a child of my age – which is to say a perfect hypocrite – I heed the summons. The brief is simple. We are to make a programme and I am to present it. I am to be the frontperson.

The message comes through: meet the rest of the crew at a certain house in the North of London, on a certain day, at a certain time. Naturally, I am late. To be early signifies keenness and keenness, in our age, is not to be trusted. Also, I am a little drunk. Also, I am in a foul mood. I think I just about loathe everything in life. I scowl at children, swear at pretty women, curse the sky, shout at the young, shoulder the old. In a strange sort of way this makes me happy; it makes me free. My loathing gives me pleasure; it makes me safe. It is the truest thing about me.

I therefore have a few more drinks at a couple of pubs on the way and by the time I arrive I am in a stinking funk, a perfect peach of a foul mood. I'm in a splendid state to see the worst in everything. And what is more, I enjoy this acidic perception, this delicious jaundice. The mind never works so well as when it means to see everything so ill. A nasty frame of mind has something almost artistic about it. True refinement requires the delicate veiling of malice. I think I'm one of the most refined people I know.

And so, beautifully primed, I swagger in to the meeting.

Three

They were all there, gloomy in their failures. What a crew! One look at them and the heart revives. The sea writhes with sinking ships. What a joy to behold, all six of them, all clinging on by their broken fingernails to the rotten beams of hope. All sad cases. First there was Jim, squat and fat and balding. He is the director, the director in the last chance saloon. Hadn't directed a film or indeed anything in at least seven years. God knows how he got this job. Incompetent beyond description. Responsible for the worst films on earth, or in hell. I've always said that when the devil wants to punish film critics he makes them watch Jim's entire cannon. From beginning to end. Every day. Every night. Without remission. That's hell. And that's Jim for you. It must be a joke. A setup. Can't explain it otherwise.

Then there's Propr. The sound man. Totally unsound. Practically deaf, tone deaf, that is. Has all the equipment. Complete fanatic about noise. Goes crazy about the slightest sound ten miles away, but spends all his time listening to garbage. Thin, wiry, gobble-eyed, scrawny-necked sound fanatic. Hasn't worked on a film for five years. Been working with sheep up in the North somewhere, on an allotment. Worst sound man ever. Was voted the worst sound man three times, three years consecutively, by the Academy. Was eventually thrown out, but folks kicked up a fuss on account of his long service to the industry and he was let back in. Often seen at the Academy bar, propping up a drink on his moustache. Hence the name. No one ever talks to him. He's the only sound man who creates no echoes. There are people who are invisible. That is they are so insignificant that no one notices them. This guy Propr is inaudible. If he hollers no one hears him. Perfect for the job. A joke, a divine joke. He's the sound man, dragged out of the backwaters. Marvellous.

And for researcher and general organiser we have Husk. She's thin, nervy, sour, grim, prim, rat-eyed, and almost admirable. Except that she's obsessed. With money. With losing weight. With flies. She's obsessed with being obsessed. She's mad, of course, but Jim has a thing about her. Jim's sweet on her in some way, so, of course, here she is, on the team. She's worked on a film recently. Like yesterday. She's always working. On complete rubbish, of course. All the dead-end television shows. All the trial runs that never have a future. Anything. If there's a camera involved, and it might accidentally project something onto a television screen, then you can be sure that Husk will want to be involved. All the most menial tasks. The drudgery tasks. The dead-beat jobs. You've got to admire her. There's something heroic about her stupidity. If it weren't for those rat-like eyes of hers, I'd quite fancy her, if only for her obsession and for the stink of failure that floats about her like a faded perfume. On some people failure is positively an aphrodisiac.

When I'm in this mood I exaggerate, I distort; but we never tell the truth so much as when we exaggerate and distort. When I'm in this mood I do everyone an injustice, I assassinate their characters, I lie, I twist things, and what is more I enjoy it. We tell the truth more when we're telling lies than when we're telling the truth. I don't trust people when they say they are telling the truth. But it's possible to tell lies, and to let truth smuggle itself in. Everyone, in shadow, has the vices we ascribe to them. All perception is superstitious. All perception is false. All perception is true.

How many of the crew have I mentioned now? Three. Three more to go. I'll hurry through them. First, there's Riley, the assistant cameraman, actually a woman, actually a man-girl. Strangest creature I every saw. Don't quite know how to describe her. Small, wiry, full of a mad squirrel-like amphetamine-driven panic-charged vaguely neurotic energy. Nice eyes. I hate to admit it, but nice eyes. I like them. I adore them. Charming, sweet, pretty eyes. Can't make out how a weirdo gets to have such nice eyes. Nice smile too, when she finds it. Sort of knocks your eyeballs and your cynicism sideways when she smiles. The mind reels, like being kissed by the person you most secretly fancy, and you think: wow, where did that smile come from? Cranky energy. The sort of energy that some orphans have. Compensating wildly, of course. For something or other. More energy than sense. Dane. The most un-Danish person I ever met. Scatty, boyish, like an urchin, like one of those street kids out of Fagin's gang in *Oliver Twist*. But not as likeable. Too scatty, smiles too much, when the mood takes her. People who smile too much make me nervous. Something mad about it. Only the mad smile like that. The mad, or the stupid, or the chronically insecure. Only a fool wants everyone to like them. Only a fool wants to please everyone. Only the mad think they can do both. She makes me nervous. Hasn't worked in film or TV for ages. Therefore desperate. Anxious to please. Can't stand those who are anxious to please. They should be flogged. Have some sense flogged into them. Who do they want to please anyway? They want to please those who will devour them, or who will never notice them, or who despise them precisely because of their efforts to please. Who wants to please the arseholes that run and ruin the world? The bosses, the chiefs, the directors, the head of this corporation or that business, who gives a toss, it's all egotism and emptiness anyway, and only perverts go out of their way to try and please them. So there's her. Trying too hard. Smiling herself sort of stupid. I avoid her completely, and snarl when she says hello.

Next, there's the first cameraman. Talkative. How he talks. His mother must have taken a vow of silence during the nine months of pregnancy. Now he's inflicting vengeance on the world. God spare our ears. Can't figure out why those who talk the most have the least to say. There are certain faulty village taps in Africa that never stop running. They wear out the stone beneath them on which the villagers rest their buckets. The stones are hollowed within weeks. The first cameraman is like that. He hollows you out with his ceaseless flow of words. They call him Sam. God knows why he's got such a simple name. He'd drive you to suicide or murder with his talk. Some people eat to live, others live to eat. Sam lives to talk, and talks to live. That's why he's so thin. Talks away everything, his money, his intelligence, his energy, his relationships, his mind... He's the first person who made me realise that you can talk away your vital powers, that to talk too much is to drain yourself. Those that the gods want to render stupid they first make talkative. That's the way it is. This verbal insanity drains people around him, for there is something of the vacuum cleaner effect about listening to someone who never stops talking. They seem to dissipate your vital powers too. They dull the mind, dampen the spirits, and leave you somewhat comatose, like a hare caught in a headlight. There is a sort of hallucination induced by listening politely to someone who goes on for ever. Politeness is a kind of perversity, and overly polite people deserve what they get. But apart from this unfortunate propensity, an absolute curse in a cameraman, Sam is pleasant enough, which is to say his imbecility is charming, God knows why. He's like one of those insane babies that nature protects with a sweet nature and filthy rich parents. He has the blessed nitrogen of enthusiasm, unforgivable in any other occupation but that of a cameraman, a job that borders on the absurd anyway – risking a life to capture ephemera – that only a holy fool or, better still, an unholy fool, lifts it into something worthwhile. And Sam would spend a month in a sewer to capture an image. He would sleep in a marshland to bring home a good shot. In fact, the more asinine the project, the more punishment involved, the more humiliation, the more enthusiastic Sam becomes. There is more than a whiff of medieval penance in his immersions. Which is why it is so puzzling that he's taken on a tame job like this. No bogs here. No coal mines. No sewers. No mountain crags. Just a straightforward train journey to some forgotten place in Greece. Then I remember his mouth. He has alienated just about every film-maker in town. Driven a few quite mad. Folks flee him. No one will employ him because he bores crews silly. Hasn't done proper work for years. Still a young man. But looks old. Talking too much has aged him. Someone should lock him up in a Trappist monastery. We're stuck with him for three weeks. Unless he undergoes a conversion. Or falls in love. With a perfect listener.

Then, finally, to round off the core of the crew, there's Jute. Never seen her before, but when I first clap eyes on her I automatically nickname her The Spy. The eyes and ears of Big Brother. Listening to everything. Sees everything. Expresses no opinions. Expresses no emotions. Face like a bucket of water. Expressionless as a mirror, as a book without a cover. But beneath the expressionlessness, a terrible mask of inflexible judgement, a Northern severity, an absolute moral sternness. Her gaze makes you uncertain about the condition of your underwear. Her look makes you doubt the health of your bowels. People who address her don't speak clearly, because they fear her silent judgement of their dental hygiene. Everything about her is terrifyingly neat. She's a

Gorgon of moral rectitude, a Medusa of propriety. Humourlessness never had a grimmer face. She makes one think of those people who have had pitiless and joyless childhoods, whose entire adult life is one long revenge against all those who laughed as children. She's in the team clearly to make sure that we have absolutely no fun. She's the controller of our meagre initial purse, she's our movable accountant, the organisation incarnate, with a fresh rule book always to hand, readily consulted. One can only pray that she gets kidnapped. Otherwise, it's like having all the things you ever revolted against, the strictures of school, the intolerant headmistress, the echoing corridors of dreadful institutions, the cabal of Chinese whisperers, the lifelong killjoys, all rolled into one fanatical obeyer of corporation edicts. That's who we've got supervising our escape from our failures and just about everything else.

There's the six, an incompetent crew, a crew from hell. If we don't murder one another, we'll create a new religion.

Four

It turns out, however, that they've all changed since I last saw them. I didn't notice it straight away. We never notice such changes straight away, we just go on treating people according to the way we have always thought of them. A wonderful failing, I think. We hate the idea of people changing. Anyway, they'd mostly changed, some for the worse, some for the better, some merely adding on more weirdnesses to the ones they had already. I can't say I know them any more. But I'll let my impressions stand, because that's how we see people, in an unchanging past tense, and that's how we measure their changes. And so, at the time, they were still the same old faces to me. And I was still the same old bastard to them. Maybe I too had changed without knowing it. We are always the last to know.

Five

The meeting proceeds. Folks talk to one another. I talk to no one. I scowl by the window, staring out into grim grey suburbia. The slate coloured light of the world fits my soul perfectly. I drink in the delectable juice of my own malaise. They all talk behind me, about filming schedules, stop-off points, countries, hotels, bookings, traveller's cheques, conversion rates, all the tedious logistics of low-budget films. They talk loud enough for me to hear. They know it's the only way to convey information to me. Who can withstand my scorn when I'm sitting in it like a pasha on silk cushions? Compared to my flaming acid spirit, Iago is a slug. Even dogs behold me in my meaner moods and rear back, howling. I pride myself on being able to generate such horror. This, I think, is a major achievement. It takes a peculiar courage to inflict one's mean-spiritedness on the world – especially on a world where phoneyness rules, phoney warmth, phoney friend-ships, phoney sympathies. I want to scorch them all with pure distilled contempt. I've become my own alchemist.

But as I stand at the window, trying to crack the pane with my expression, some of the things I hear, filtering across on whispered tones, make me wake up slowly. That may have been the first time that my cynicism came to the rescue. It was the first time that I sensed that within our journey there was another secret journey, a cryptic journey. Our trip was a pretext for some-thing else, and that something had to do with the much whispered name, Malasso...

What is it about certain names that upon first hearing them they conjure a fate, a story, a malediction, a misadventure, a misfortune crouched just ahead of you like a road that has turned suddenly into a gigantic cobra? What is it about certain names, whispered in a certain way, that makes you suddenly aware of dangers ahead, of hairpin bends that lead straight over precipices the colour of perfect midnight? Names that make you think of perils in the evening, of the glint of a gun at night, of a blade and the warm smell of blood, of treachery slashing the soft flesh of your belly with a warm and sinister smile? Such were the effects of the susurrations of that name...

But before I could turn round, or ask a question, the conversation moved on to practical things. Itineraries. Tickets. Laundry arrangements. And then a gentle litany of magic names, place-names; vowels and consonants that, for a moment, lisped past the fortress of my impregnable cynicism, and wove a feathery enchantment over the little boy who once dreamt of flying with his own wings to all the lovely places in the world, places whose beauty was compacted into their names. I listened, and heard, briefly, something new, in the hidden landscapes. Waterloo... Exilus... Eden... Paris... Babylon... Utopia... Versailles... Atlantis... Arcadia...

Six

Maybe I slept. Maybe I dreamt. Maybe the words cast a yellow spell over my mind. The names set me dreaming, a little. And I was a little boy again, with a red train, travelling across the green oceans of the spherical world at the speed of my own willing. Atlases dissolved into landscapes, and the revolving orb became my journey in space, round the lives of millions, unseen from the moon. But the names set me to dreaming, and brought me back to earth again, and set me to cursing. I went and got a beer from the fridge, and scowled, and berated everyone, and was generally foul, and the worse I got the more I knew that the names had got to me. There's nothing makes a man more mean-spirited than when his malice has been set in flight, charmed into lightness.

I made damn well sure they all paid for it, and gave myself a fine ugly reputation all round, and topped it up for those that didn't know me already and framed it in gold for those that did.

But the charm had worked. Before I knew it I was rehearsing the journey, swearing all the while, spraying beer at the sound man, breathing my disgusting fumes on Jute the inflexible. The cameraman made a few trial shots, and muttered something about my profile having become more noble for my greater biliousness. This, of course, enraged me; and my rage delighted them. And so my hostility towards the camera crystallised. I became convinced that it was a spy, certain that it was not so much a faithful recorder of what it captured as a distorter of what it gazed upon. No one with any intelligence has ever had a truly comfortable relationship with that abstract piece of technology. It is a cyclopean head without a brain, with an eye that gazes insensibly upon what it witnesses. It is a piece of technology for the magnification of the ego, the multiplication of unreality. It stares on corpses as on flowers with the same mindless equanimity. It devours light. It feeds the eyeballs pointless images, it has an inflexible point of view, and it is the greatest disseminator of illusions. In a world already composed, atom by atom, of illusions (the illusion that what we perceive is the true reality) you can see how this instrument tyrannises the minds of men and women.

How strange, phoney, self-conscious, greedy, egotistical, and childish people become when a camera is trained upon them, offering their feeble minds the illusion of fame – of fame, that most unexamined of monsters, that most fabulous of sirens, that devourer of true time and true living, that deceiver, ruiner, that externaliser of fantasies. To yield to the camera and its hidden promise of transforming your life through the multiplication of your image, to yield to it, like a whore, a pervert, like a pathological exhibitionist, like a stripper, is a shameless confession of imbecility. It is to concede that your true worth and measure reside only and absolutely in the eyes of others; it is to concede that you don't exist till you are indeed seen on the screen. It is to collude in the invalidation of your natural flesh-and-blood life; it is to render yourself impotent, unhistorical, non-existent, marginal, a eunuch of time, a cipher of space, a non-person; it is to accept the notion not so much *cogito ergo sum* as *in camera ergo sum*, a monstrous reduction of self from selfhood to visibility-hood. The logical conclusion therefore that an intelligent person can reach is the one reached by me on that miserable day – which is that the camera is one of the devil's spies. It looks into your external ego and reports to the mighty corporation of the diabolical that here is another lump of meat ready for processing in the vast factories of celluloid hell; that here is someone willing to make a pact with the great witty prince of the dark, a pact in which the image of their most perishable aspects is traded for the mysterious animation of their life; that here is one cheap to buy, cheap at the price, an image for a soul.

I had developed a tremendous hatred for the camera; and the more it flattered me and seduced me with the lying images of beauty, of a splendid profile concocted out of my celebrated bad-temperedness, the more I loathed that machine of egotism. And so that day, while we went through our trial runs, and saw what pleasant images of me it produced, the more difficult I became, the more refractory. This gave me much pleasure indeed, a pleasure spoilt by the curious discovery that there is nothing the camera likes so much as a refractory subject. As with a true courtesan, the more resistance there is to overcome, the more fascinated the camera becomes, the more there is to show, to see. A dynamic is set up. Will egotism triumph over coyness, over unwillingness? The camera becomes riveted, it becomes gleeful. If you look hard enough you can sometimes catch the camera slobbering, no, salivating, in preternatural lust, over a vista of corpses, over disasters, famine, plagues, transgressions, deviancies, monstrosities, horrors. It looks on evil with a glint in its eye. When it lingers on beauty that's because it wants to violate it, and when it dwells on innocence it does so with concealed cynicism. Sentimentality delights the camera, for sentimentality is a distortion and conceals a vague monstrosity. The devil gazes on the world with beady eyes; and the meaning of its gaze is more ambiguous than death, more menacing than a vile hidden intention. There is a ghoul in every camera that feeds on living flesh, and only the wise or the lucky subvert the spy and the ghoul, feeding one lies that reveal truth and feeding the latter dying flesh that it may, unintentionally, yield living revelations.

If one must work for the devil, then one must be an unpleasant servant, a servant that wants to overthrow the master, and gain the sublime laughter of liberation. But who understands these things in this world of blockheads and literal minds, in a world where people thoughtlessly believe what they read, accept what they see, and are convinced by everything they hear. I could be lying to you now and you'd believe it because I say it is thus. And so I play the game of revolving meanings, the double and triple bluff, and leave you enraged at an enigma that does not speak the plain idiotic language that you are used to, the language by which politicians and admen con you, the language of so-called plain speaking that blinds you to the lies you are fed, the language that makes a sheep out of you. If you cannot read me inside out, like a riddle or a paradox, how will you ever make sense of the invisible inscriptions? I hope I'm getting on your nerves. I hope I'm infuriating you so much that you want to throw this book aside and pick up one more suited to your sheep-like complacency. Actually, I don't mind sheep. It's human beings behaving like sheep that I can't stand. I hope this is getting through to you. I don't want any complacent bastards on this journey. There are enough of those as it is. We are drawing up to the next station, a chapter ending. You can get off and bugger off if you don't want to continue. But don't ask for your money back. I've spent it.

Seven

Every now and again life sends us little messages. The messages are meant for us alone. No one else can see them. No one else perceives them as messages. They may seem perfectly banal to the world, but to you, for whom they were intended, they have the force of revelation. Much of the failure and success of a life, much of the joy or suffering in a life, depends on being able to see these secret messages. And much of the magic, or tragedy of life depends on being able to decipher and interpret these messages. Those who spend their lives over-deciphering tend to go mad, they go round the bend, they become paranoid; and every billboard and scrap of paper which the wind blows their way, or every other image or word called out on a television screen becomes a message of overwhelming importance to them. Then the messages drive out living, drive out life. But those who live their lives without seeing the messages at all, or seeing them but not deciphering them, or not interpreting them properly, live dumb lives, perpetually adrift on the barren seas of mediocrity and insignificance, the deadly boring wastes of orthodoxy. In short, they have no dialogue with the universe or with themselves.

There is nothing more scary than when a cynic starts to prophesy. Nothing more hair-raising than when the blind can see. This world is upside-down, inside-out, my friend. What is real is unreal, what's unreal is real. Sometimes my mind scares me. Sometimes one gets a notion about the world that's too great to think through. For, sometimes, messages come from behind the veil of living. Sometimes an inscription appears in the quotidian which is an important road sign in your life. They appear right there in the midst of the most ordinary moments. Don't ask me where the messages come from. Don't ask me where the inscriptions come from. Maybe we just see them because they are right for us. Maybe we see them because we need to, because we've been too blind to what life is trying to tell us. How the hell should I know. Belshazzar saw his in the midst of a splendid feast. A hand inscribed his message on a wall. Other people have seen signs in altered states, and read the wrong inscriptions, or didn't interpret them right. They come in a thousand ways. They come in daily life, in as many forms as there are ways of reading the world. They take the form of symbols, of words, of something heard, or whispered in one's head. They are blown over by the wind. They appear in the sky, or stand out suddenly in a book one is reading, or a painting one is staring at absent-mindedly, or a piece of music not listened to but heard in a mysterious new way. They are there and then they are gone. Like a flash of lightning not seen but sensed. Something made clear. Then made dark again. Some people say that the universe is a constant message to us anyway, a message of startling simplicity. The simplicity of the greatest riddle or paradox. I don't know about all that. Too deep for me, I think. All I can say for sure is that there is a mysterious veil that separates the living from the others. And this veil is made of perception. And don't ask me who the others are. They may be the dead. Except that the dead are not dead: they are just not alive in bodies. They may be angels, guardian angels, sinners and cynics that we are. They may be one's potent and powerful ancestors, shaking their heads in sadness at the enormous blunders we are making in our lives. They may be illumined beings. Who can say yeah or nay? They may sometimes even be demons, messengers of the devil, who uses as many tricks to get to us as there are devices to save us. All I know is that there is a veil, and messages are projected through this veil. Inscriptions appear on the fabric of the world. We live in an unreality. We live in a celluloid universe. We live in a world quivering with illusion. Most of what we see just isn't there. Most of the things we feel and touch aren't there the way we think they are. Most of what is there we don't see. Most of the things that touch us don't feel. There may be things more real than us behind the invisible veil of reality. And our world, as on a cinema screen, can be one in which messages are flashed, projected. Maybe we flash the messages, maybe we project them. But their meaning is left for us to decipher. This is true too of dreams, the cinema of the universal interior, the celluloid of sleep. But I'm not talking about that right now. I'm talking about the little secret messages that life sends us, sends to us alone.

That day, with the dreadful crew gathered in that appalling suburban flat (of which the owner was inordinately proud), I received one of those messages. I don't know where it came from. I don't know who passed it to me. Everyone there absolutely denied having had anything to do with it. But it appeared in my palm, while I was raging against the camera. The message was typed on a piece of red paper. And it read: Beware the inscription.

Eight

That is when the name Malasso first sounded on our journey. I told no one at all about the message. But when no one claimed responsibility for having planted it, a voice from out of nowhere suggested that the message might have come from Malasso. There was a peculiar silence after that.

'Who is Malasso?' I asked.

No one said anything. Everyone returned immediately to their tasks. For the first time that day my mood changed. I entered a different emotional zone. It was as if an illness had crept into my blood through my ears. My energy levels changed as well. There are certain names, with their inscrutable syllables, or their suppressed and diabolical vowels, that have the power to make you ill, or to lose your memory, or to forget what love is, or to distort your vision, or to send you spiralling, in encoded dread, towards some ambiguous doom.

I took it then, from their silence, that Malasso was not a name to mention at all, if it could be helped. There are certain peoples who invent a character to explain all the inexplicable mishaps and disasters and tragedies that befall them. These characters are responsible for the failures of harvests and for clothes missing from washing lines and manholes being left open and burglaries with no break-ins and road signs facing the wrong way. When a house mysteriously burns down, they say it was Procous that did it (Procous being the name of this imaginary semi-deity of disasters, mischief, local catastrophes, lost things, improbable thefts, and unlikely rumours). In our case, it seemed as if the crew had invented such a figure to explain lifts that wouldn't open on the fifteenth floor, missing schedules, disasters in the air, money that vanished, stations that never existed, and all the finely calibrated tortures of the adventures ahead. They were all caused by Malasso. That was at first what I took it to mean; and I adjusted my inner being to make space for the presence of this mysterious force in our lives, this malign Prospero figure who would have such dreadful power over our lives as we travelled on towards that illusory goal of Arcadia. I made space for this new fiend, and I asked no further questions for the time being, and didn't mention his name any more. But I confess that with the receiving of the message something changed in me, something that had always been there.

I sometimes believe that when God wants to turn your life around he puts more of the devil in you. My life was being turned upside-down, and a strange kind of daemon had awoken in me, making more keen the edge of my perceptions. I was, as they say, not myself. There are certain men in Africa who shake hands with you and afterwards you don't feel well. There are certain people in Africa who give you peculiar objects, and once these objects touch your palm a sleeping paranoia awakens in you, and washing your hands a thousand times with carbolic soap or herbal potions can't rid you of the sensation of being spooked. These are travellers' tales which I happen to believe, being intelligent. So it was with the message that was passed on to me. I wasn't the same afterwards. I was never the same again.

Nine

I became obsessed. The curious nature of my obsession became clearer to me only much later. At first it manifested itself as a kind of vague irritability, the invidious irritability that specialists in psychosomatic creativity identify as preceding unusual irradiations of perceptivity. In simpler words, I became more sensitive than usual. It is a common misunderstanding that bad-tempered types are impervious people, thick-skinned, insensitive. It may be nearer to the truth, in some cases, to say that they are hypersensitive, but not fey, merely more sensitive to the coarse material of everyday life, to the brutish fabric of day to day dealings, of commonplace politeness, of average good manners. It seems to me that most people who are not bad-tempered, who are even-keeled, mediocre in their tranquillity – are the true insensitive ones. The wonderful possibilities of life brush past them without so much as stirring vague impulses of a greater way of being, a rage at the limitations that so much of society imposes on their sense of the unsuspected sublimity of being human. To have this sense lurking in you, and to find no way of expressing it, or living its fire, can either make a raging *homo sapiens* of you, or turn you towards the excessive sensitivity that can only, at best, incline towards the monastery.

My obsession took, at first, a curious form. I became aware of words heard out of context, and invested them with more meaning than could have been intended. I became a hunter after floating words. Things overheard started off complex trains of thought, of fantasy. I began to weave whole fantasies out of these hanging words. Take, for example, my overhearing some of the crew members talking. The word TREASURE drifted across to me; I froze, and listened harder. Who had mentioned it? What treasure? I began to suspect that, hidden in the agenda of our journey, was something that had to do with treasure. It didn't take long for me to put the two mysteries together: Malasso and treasure. *Voilà*. Our journey was overtly to find Arcadia, but covertly to find hidden, illegal treasure, with Malasso as the invisible *metteur en scène*. I mentioned nothing of my suspicions, but kept a closer eye on all the team members. They became enormously interesting to me for the first time in all the years I had known them. They gained in menace, in untrustworthiness, in depth. These were thorough failures, desperate media people, haunted by the marvellous and crushing contempt that the great goddess of fame had heaped on them, haunted by their complete inability to make any sort of mark on the vile fabric of the age. They were, therefore, willing accomplices of the corporation of the devil, desperadoes of fame and urban fortune. I had no reason to think them incapable of anything. Once one glimpses a person's ruling failures, without seeing anything of a counter-balancing ruling principle, then that person becomes plain. One sees clearly their capacity for mild evils, evils that can slide, slowly, into greater ones. There was no reason, to my mind, why the crew wouldn't sell me to cutthroats, if it would favour them. I had reached the finest zone of my honed paranoia. For the first time, the journey began to stimulate my keenest appetite for life, and adventure.

Ten

There was something else I noticed on that day of our trial run through the logistics of filming. I noticed that, not long after I received my special message, most of the other crew members started to act strange. This too was clearer to me much later. The schedule that we were supposed to be discussing, for example, revealed itself to be patchy. Our journey depended on nebulous instructions to be received at various future points, in various cities. Someone, in Italy or France or Greece, would disburse the necessary funds to us when we got there. All this was very peculiar, and downright unprofessional. But it was, apparently, a way of saving money, of making better use of favourable exchange rates, and so on. And then it turned out that we had to meet someone in Paris who would give Jim clear instructions; and that this person would leave clues and hints as to the next point of our journey, the next collecting place, the next man or woman to meet, the next complicated interview. All this would be communicated to Jim as we went along.

I began to feel strongly under the influence of people I didn't know. I felt I was in a bad movie. I expressed myself very severely to all the crew members on the vileness of this haphazard way of dragging us across Europe, on a pointless journey, to clandestine meetings with shady people, following tentative hints, lugging cameras and equipment around, as if we were refugees from good sense and proper methods of film-making. I protested loudly and drunkenly. I swore and cursed. I insulted the director and foamed and stamped, and they heard me out with mournful expressions. And when I had fairly talked myself out, as it were, Jim called me aside and told me, in that mild-mannered, irritating whisper of his which brings me out in a maniacal fury, that we simply had no choice.

'This is our only chance. Our last chance,' he said lugubriously. 'We either take it or leave it. We either go for it and try and make a good film, or we all go home now, and forget the whole thing.'

Put like that the ever-vigilant pragmatist in me came creeping out. We had no choice. We were the original last-chance-salooners, the cream of the bottom of the heap. We were all desperate, me as much as anyone else – hence my coruscating judgement. Yes, we had no choice, no hope, but to accept the terms presented and make the best of them.

Mad as it may sound, we took our chance. We cowered. We accepted. We plunged forward.

And so, miserable and downcast, with a sense of doom and a whiff of the abyss, and with the gloomy courage that starving rats have, we dispersed for the day, having agreed to meet again at an appointed hour, on an appointed day, at Waterloo Station.

Eleven

The world lay motionless in the golden spell of summer. The deep shade beneath the trees, the blinding fingers of sunlight, the windless warmth, the humidity that causes a peculiar ennui in the city, the dazed look of sweating commuters, the traffic fumes, the distracted tourists, the impassive grandeur of the city's architecture, the leaves of trees caught in summer's yellow enchantment, the childhood dreams of happier times by the seaside, the faded hopes of adulthood, the failed loves, the collapsed ambitions, time's merciless betrayal of our youthful certainties of becoming one of the masters of the world, the elusive nature of success and happiness, of a life with work and fun in rightful measure, the faintly disreputable middle-class aspirations now in their death-throes on summer's splendid lawns of life's ironies – these are the sweet poisonous sensations that accompany you homewards as evening draws nigh, with the sun still deceptively high in the heavens. Mariners must know this feeling, this sinking feeling, of islands glimpsed from a long distance, receding, dissolving into the fata morganas of the sea.

Oh, how life bites those who did not set out early, with stoutness of heart, and single-mindedness of intention, and a certain invaluable stupidity of soul, the stupidity that makes you pursue society's truest measure with all bullishness and crudity, with shamelessness. Oh, to be too sensitive to fight for the vulgar things of life, and then to find that the vulgarity is the very stuff that makes life in society possible; to find, too late, that the vulgarity has a hidden sublimity to it, the sublimity of leisure, of holidays, of social freedom, freedom from the awful slavery of being poor, and taking a load of nonsense from the rich, who freely admit to their superiority, the wonderful superiority of being stupid enough to put the least important things in life absolutely first – which is to say the healthy, robust, and the utterly fascinating pursuit of money, the grovelling slavering slobbering greed and lust for it, the barbaric gloating for it, the superhuman translation of all the finest energies and intelligence in the human spirit into an unholy scrum and scree for money, the gagging gasping frothing passionate crawling for money, wherever it can legitimately, or quasi-legitimately, be found, and accumulated. For here the gorgeous vengeance begins; the price has been paid; and all those who didn't pay the price, make the effort, who didn't bleed and beg and lick and stab for it deserve their unfreedom, their slavery, their unbearable airless lives, their despondency, their rat-like psychotic resentment, their bitterness and bile, their horrible envy, and their dreadful stinking powerlessness.

Oh, but it was nonetheless summer, and the world was all abreath with the glory of the fine season come round at last with the great benediction of light everywhere spreading delicious warm throbs of lust in the blood of the young girls and the beautiful women who are now all out and transformed from their sylph-like slenderness, their unripeness, into absolute desirousness. Oh, desire was abroad, and love was dancing in the air, cavorting along the invisible passion pylons that connect us all in a gaze. And where desire can find no hope, wracked by poor self-esteem, oh, how summer fills you with an impossible longing and resentment, an envy for all those who are in love and who are just being devoured by the great illusion of it all, the illusion of life's fairytale, of happy resolutions in the midst of living, when in living there are no resolutions at all, as any intelligent person will tell you, but only the tangled tale that goes on...

In the throes of these tangles, I beheld the world spinning in summer's richness as I made my way back home. And it occurred to me, amid the dissatisfactions of life, that maybe my screaming nerves had a secret resonance with this forthcoming journey. Besides, I had to start thinking and feeling my way into the journey's theme. When one's life is a chaos one only seeks more chaos if what one really seeks is oblivion. But no matter how awful I feel things to be, I don't want oblivion just yet. I want to hurl a few marvellous surprises into the great jaws of life. I want myself to be the surprise. I don't want to spend the rest of my life stewing in bile. I too dream of a workable resolution, but I can't seem to find the will to straighten things out. I can't seem to go forward, therefore I must go back. I must find the lost beginnings, must reincarnate childhood, find a new reason for breathing, make a new covenant. I must find a way to make death not a threat, an enemy, a terror, an excuse, but a friend, an aid, a liberator. For it would seem that death is the golden key to the mystery of living, but I don't know how to use it. And so, raging or not, hypocrite or not, loathing the camera or not, cynic or not, I need this journey. I need to find out what reasons other people have for living. I need to be broken down again into the simplest components and re-assembled like a beautiful jigsaw into a more lovely picture of who I really am and what I can be.

Slowly, I was learning to love my theme. Hello to journeys. *Salut* to escapes. I hope my escape leads me back to myself, by a new route, so that I can see my life and its possibilities as if for the first time.

And so this journey must be a sort of dying for me; a dying of the old self; a birth of something new and fearless and bright and strange.

BOOK TWO

One

They had all lost something. All the voyagers at the station, young or old, had lost something. It was on their faces. It was written there, like secret inscriptions. The camera could see it; could see the anxiety and stress, the loneliness, the odd vacancy that precedes a journey. And when the camera saw it, Jim sensed it too. With his hair practically falling out, he directed Sam to focus on the faces, and to do it so that they wouldn't notice.

Waterloo Station was crowded. But much more than the crowding of people was the crowding of anxiety and stress. It was palpable. Seen through the demonic eye of the camera it was curiously terrifying, like a hidden growth that has been there all along and suddenly springs into visibility. Death was chewing us all up, devouring us, bit by bit, beginning first with the intangible parts of us, our psyches, our childhoods, our futures, our hopes, the time we had left on this planet.

All around, the crew members were performing their different tasks. Husk was busying herself with the clapperboard, running between me and the director. Propr was taking sound levels with his muffled microphone. Jute was making phone calls to mysterious superiors, reporting on the progress of things; Sam was wielding his devil's instrument, and I was waiting. And not far from me, among the crowd, was my friend, Mistletoe, a red-haired painter, whom I had asked to accompany me, if she had nothing better to do, because I was certain I would need saving from myself.

The day hadn't begun well. Significant journeys rarely do. There was the business with the lift, a precursor of worse disasters to come. I could smell the hand of Malasso in it. The crew had taken a lift up a nearby building to get aerial shots of London. On the thirteenth floor, or thereabouts, the lift had come to a halt, and the crew had been trapped in the tiny space for the best part of forty minutes. Sam had fainted, Jute had become hysterical, Propr had maintained a silent stoicism, Riley had fretted and twitched, Jim had kept his nerve but lost more of his hair; and the photographer who was with them smiled, and smiled; God knows why. And I – I was having a drink downstairs in the station bar. Those whom the devil don't love, well, they get drunk and slip through his net. I saw them all an hour later. They were much dehydrated, profoundly spooked, and exceedingly humourless. You can imagine my quiet delight. I think I ordered another drink for myself.

Two

But I was bothered by what I saw in the station. I think the drunkenness helped. I saw faces lost in a labyrinth, lost in the dark woods of reality. I saw fear lurking beneath youthful certainty, saw care eating the flesh beneath age, and horror walking beside every shadow. No one was alone. They had all brought their baggage with them, their real baggage and their psychic baggage. They had brought their ghosts with them, had brought their fears, their failures, the problems that had haunted their fathers, the nightmares that troubled their mothers. I saw a host of invisible others, writhing in their beings, sitting on their heads, entangling their feet, distorting their smiles, weighing down their minds, clinging to their necks like lovers. It was so terrifying a sight that I began to suspect the beer.

We never travel alone. An extended family of unacknowledged monsters follow us. And they don't die with us; they become part of our children.

Suddenly I knew why I wanted to make the film, or rather why the film wanted us to make it. The theme had chosen, in the true perversity of all real themes, the most unlikely, the most incompetent, and the most hopeless of people to realise something that the most competent would never think worth saying, or showing. There is a wonderful comedy in a great theme sounding its notes through the most unworthy subjects, or artists.

And it was the horror that hides in all journeys that leapt out at me that morning on Waterloo Station.

Three

The crew had lost its sense of humour; and I was beginning to find my sense of purpose. There was some agitation amongst the crew members. Filming had to be briefly halted. Jute was semi-hysterical, and Jim was trying to quieten her down. At first I assumed that they hadn't quite recovered from the horror of being stuck in the lift. I stood there a while, looking at the mild frenzy of the travellers milling up and down the concourse, dragging their luggage, glancing anxiously up at the clock or up at the giant destination board. I dawdled. The hidden horror beneath journeys yawned in front of me. I was about to go and get myself another beer, while the commotion among the crew settled, when I saw Jim summoning me, waving frantically. I hurried over and learnt, to my surprise, that Jute had received, in her palm, from a completely unknown source, a blood-red piece of paper just like the one I had found on me. She too had received a message. She had read the message, was horrified by it, and knew she couldn't possibly show it to anyone else. She stood there, surrounded by the entire crew, with the red message in her hand, looking round frantically and suspiciously at everyone, unable to believe that she had been slipped the note without being aware of it.

'Surely you must know when you got it?' said Husk impatiently.

'Yeah, I would,' said Sam.

'You said you found it in your hand. So think back. When was your palm last empty? Was it in the lift, was it just now? It would help if you tried to remember.'

But Jute wouldn't try; she just stared at us all as if she had suddenly found herself in a nightmare.

'What does the note say?' asked Propr.

'We don't know,' replied Jim. 'She won't say.'

'This has happened before, hasn't it? It happened to you, Lao, didn't it? What did your note say? You never told us.'

'It didn't say anything that's anyone's business but my own. Everyone should attend to their own nightmares and not go sniffing around in other people's. And if you ain't got no nightmares, acquire some. I'm off to get a drink.'

And so saying, I was gone. I went to the nearest bar, ordered, and drank. Mistletoe came and joined me. I got her an orange juice. We were silent.

The bustle of arrivals and departures was everywhere. Odd to see such whirling despair. The air fairly quivered. For every traveller there was a whole train of other people, invisible people, that they had brought with them. They were dragging their dead, their ghosts, their monsters, their etiolated shadows along with them, along with their luggage. I didn't know that the world was so densely populated. Each person seemed to have five others with them. That's what made the crowding so edgy. That's why journeys, at their beginnings, are fringed with such tensions. Some people leave their ghosts, their dead, behind on the platform. Others carry them all the way. A few acquire new ghosts on their journeys, and on their way back home. I looked and saw that our crew fairly bristled with ghosts. We had brought more shadow-beings with us than anyone else in the station, apart from the tramps and a few big shots travelling first class. Maybe that is what failure is, carrying more ghosts and shadow-beings around than one's psyche can manage. I could not tell how many I had with me, but judging by the freakish state of my mind, I must be fairly mounting with them.

Four

Our initial instruction had been quite simple. At the end of our first meeting, Jim had said:

'Let's meet under the clock.'

We hadn't met there. We had met haphazardly. They had been stranded in a lift while going up to film London from the air, and I had been early, for once, and had been wandering around, looking at faces, bumping into the restless neurotic energies of the crowd, till I had picked up so much psychic debris that I needed a drink to straighten myself out. And drinking now, in silence, pondering the crowd that seemed to replenish itself, full of individuals going nowhere except round and round, as if taking their private demons for a walk, I thought about the meeting that hadn't taken place under the clock. I'm a bit like that; I think about all manner of tangential things. I like angles and odd turnings. Straightforward things bore me. In order to think about a straightforward thing I have to somehow first make it tangential. And so I thought about us setting out on our journey from under the shadow of the great clock, and what a different journey it would have been, launched from beneath such a symbol.

It occurred to me, as I got mildly pissed, that one way or another, we all set off on the road, take to ship, steal off at dawn, catch a lift on the highway, sneak out of our houses, under the shadow of the clock. I gazed now at the great black clock of the station, with its little white markings, its time partitions, and its hour and second hands crawling or speeding round the mighty sombre disc that makes time visible, makes it go round and round. I watched as it regulated and spun and made us nervy and neurotic. I gazed, mesmerised, at that great disc, on which so many eyes were riveted; and then something happened to my mind. I think I slipped off sideways into the mythical world that lurks within the giant ice-cube, where my great white horse dwells protected under the blistering sun of an endless desert. And my mind slipped in there, into its cool interiors, its boundless worlds, and I went a-wandering in free space, in time space, amongst the playthings of the spirit, in a place where there are no ghosts, no monsters, no nightmares, no evil, no failure, no fear, but only the original world, fragments of the original world, with Eden's dawn in the air, and fresh flower fragrances, and a gentle sunlight of joy. This is the place I go to sometimes, if I'm lucky, when I'm lost in the desert. There I get to be happy amongst the first things, the first night, the first flowers, the first dew, the first thoughts, the first caress of breeze on the first living flesh, the first awakening from the first consciousness, the first blooming of the first flower, on the first garden, of the first earth, with the first thoughts of love opening in my first mind of an upright being on creation day. And it was there, in that zone, in that giant ice-cube space, concealed beneath the great white horse, that I danced among notions of the first Arcadia.

Five

Intuitions in the Garden (1)

The sun was always the same, and summer was always touched
with enchantment, and the garden was always fresh, and the
flowers in their fragrances always seduced the air. And the wind
blew over the gentle waters that had settled now. And the water
flowed round the world, engirdling the earth, majestic and
pliant, shimmering and mysterious. And the earth rumbled in
its depth, and settled into solid crust on its outward form, and
became impatient to adorn itself, so that it would look beautiful
to the eyes of eternity. And so the earth became creative, and
gave birth to trees with leaves that decorated its nakedness, and
to flowers whose petals, varied in colour, manifold in form,
waved to the loneliness of space. And the earth filled its vast-
nesses with grass and savannahs and the fine sheen of deserts
and hid hope in the desert wastes in the form of oases. And it
farmed its face with brilliant greens and blues, golds and reds,
flaming pinks and diamond emeralds. And then, alone with all
its beauty, the earth discovered the moving forms of birds and
animals and humanity, and it fell in love with them, and made
a home in its womb for them when they died, and provided
them with all they needed when they were born. And the earth
fed them, clothed them, housed them, admired their freedom
and innocence, and was pleased that though they had the stars
and galaxies, the immeasurable heavens above them, below
them they only had her, the earth, a small globe of a garden in

the fathomless reaches of the universe.

Here things bloom; things die; things are born; silence attends their beginnings and their ends. The wind wreathes the world with havoc and tenderness and songs. Freedom is woven into the fibre of things. Happiness is laced into the breathing material of all things. Love flows from the bird to the flower, and from the enigmatic calyxes to the bees and butterflies that know their language and take part in their dance. Rivers run through the dreams of the earth. Lightning separates the realms. Gods hide in all things, folding infinite forms into the tiniest spaces, dispersing their formlessness into the wind and rain, into disasters and regenerations, into the sprouting of seeds or the rotting of dead flesh, into the insubstantiality of rainclouds or the substantiality of diamonds, or the heaving of volcanoes.

Intuitions in the Garden (2)

Creation and destruction were both part of the same song. No one looked from on high to pass judgement on them. No one suffered from close by to curse them with value. Life and death were the same thing. No one mourned from on high the passing of a robin, the death of a doe, the stillbirth of a dromedary, the collapse of a man in a cave near the mountain or the expiration of a woman on the banks of a passionate river. And no one mourned from nearby either. The earth accepted its guests as it does the falling leaves of autumn, the descending spiral of a meteor, or the quiet extirpation of a worm wriggling its last within the runnels of dust.

Everything was woven of the cloth of mystery. The earth was mysterious to herself; and flowers seeded and bloomed within its own mystery, its dark timeless smile. Rivers ran and danced in space, and ribboned the earth, silvery and changeable, unique in space, harbouring its own cities and indolent fishes, deep and darkly joyful in its own mystery too. And the wind blew from the first breath, and cleansed the world roundabout, and chased the waters on, and ruffled playfully the hair of trees and bushes, and sped the gentle seeds of lazy flowers over the great distances between being born and being real; and the wind cavorted and played, danced and was free, whistled and raged, whirled and twisted, as it felt, in its own immortal mystery.

And the sky had no name; and the stars had no designation; and the deep blue of the expanse, dotted with universes, with worlds, was deep in silence too. And outwards it all opened, and there were no measurements, no songs, no hope, no fear, no emotions, no signs, no horrors, no nightmares in space, or wandering the earth. The planets glided, elided, dissolved, stewed in vapours and gases, and regarded one another, across impossible reaches, in complete silence, and without wonder. And the sky, holding such incomprehensible wonders, was itself the home of dreaming, and its vastness soon became inhabitable when the faintly awakening beings on two legs began to find the vastness unbearable in its excess of mystery, their absolute terror of the unknown and the unknowable.

Intuitions in the Garden (3)

For the great sky, surrounding the nakedness on all sides, suggested a loneliness on earth that was intolerable in the mighty Universe. A loneliness that drove animals to extinction, a loneliness that would never trouble the flowers and trees, who have contemplated the loneliness anyway and found it fruitful and enjoyed the uniqueness it conferred on their blooming and terrestrial survival.

The trees and the plants, in pondering this uniqueness in all space, fell into a state of wonder, and began to produce their most beautiful flowers, their most flavoursome fruits. They delved deep into a happiness without end, a tranquillity without measure, a serenity deeper than the oceans, and a complete ease with their living and dying.

For they knew that, at one time, they breathed and were happy in the wide universe, with nothing like them weaving their colours or exhaling their fragrances anywhere in the world of innumerable stars. And in the knowledge of their originality they suffered not from loneliness but from the very source of consolation itself, from the very origin of grace, for there is something blessed about a unique thing, a thing of wonder.

And the trees and plants, the fishes and birds were enriched with this sober contemplation, and then forgot the nature of their contemplation, but kept the result, which was a serenity, a grace, a blessed carefreeness about the nightmares and the mysteries. And they incarnated beauty in their germination and fructification. They embodied solace. They breathed out tranquillity.

They had attended at dawn to the first things, had intuited the last things, had seen how all things are blessed by the star under which they chose to live, by the thoughts they chose to dwell on, and the orientation they grew by. They had chosen, at dawn, to wonder at self's uniqueness, and happiness followed. They had chosen joy at self's existence, and freedom followed. They had chosen the love of self's regenerativeness, and prosperity followed; the necessity of self's presence, and stillness followed; the certainty of self's growth, and power followed. They had chosen the beauty of self's death, and awareness followed; the sense of self's continuance, and peace followed.

And so after the struggles of creativity, and the compensation of natural joy, nothing else concerned them. Nothing else was their business.

They left all the rest to the rest. The end of time, the beginning of things, the death of planets, the names of the force that made its sap to rise, the inclinations of the different winds, the taste of star-ash from far-flung galaxies, dying and living, these were not their business. The trees and plants, the fishes and birds, they had done all their thinking at dawn, and had the good sense to forget it all; but they lived out the results of their contemplation amongst first things, when the universe was still young.

Intuitions in the Garden (4)

And then came humanity, standing on two legs, making death into something bigger than life.

And then was born mourning, and great sorrowing, and death-mounds, and melancholy, and a terror of extinction, and a fear of the darkness, and dreadful speculations without solutions, only further speculations without end and without grace.

And then came Hades.

Then anxiety.

Then fear.

Then the fleetingness of happiness, and joy.

Then fled freedom.

Then grew the love of power, perceived antidote to dying.

Then confusion.

Then misery in the garden.

Then living became a treadmill, a thing to be endured, but not enjoyed. A thing not savoured, but soured.

Then fled our most intimate sense of immortality, the intuition that we are made of star-dust, and magic.

And then we dreamt of paradise, because we had lost it.

Six

Hysteria was bristling everywhere on the concourse of the station. The crew were in disarray, like an army that is defeated before it sets out. The shabbiness of the whole thing delighted my infernal sense of humour; and put me in a mood to celebrate the omnipresence of hysteria, and to sing a hymn to journeys that go bad before they have begun. To begin with disintegration is wonderfully hopeful, because the resultant journey is either towards the finest pits of hell, or it's a journey which can rise, by gentle gradients of unlikely grace, to a manageable kind of private heaven.

The hysteria of the crew, as hysteria generally goes, was magnetised to the point of maximum serenity, which is to say chaos, which is to say me. Jute suddenly took it into her head that she and I now had something in common because of the messages. I loathe having anything in common with anybody. It is distressing enough being human. Anyway, she came fluttering, no, storming over and asked to know what my message had said.

'None of your bloody business,' I snarled.

'But we're in this together,' she pleaded.

'No, we're not. You've got your message, and I've got mine. You've got your stuff to deal with, and so have I. Why don't you just get on with it, and leave me alone.'

'You fight alone, you die alone,' she snapped.

'I fight alone anyway; and all death is dying alone.'

'You're such a miserable bastard.'

'But I'm happier in my misery than you are in your happiness.'

She stared at me, and for the first time I saw tears sparkling in her eyes. She leant over to me and almost whispered:

'The message scares me. I can't tell you how frightened I am.'

'Messages don't kill,' I said philosophically. 'It's what we do with them that matters. I'm ignoring mine, otherwise I'd spend all my time trying to puzzle it out, and then I'd go barmy, which I am already, anyway.'

This seemed to quieten her a little, but she still seemed different. She looked as if she was facing the prospect of an execution, or torture, or abduction. She looked a little dazed, as if nothing dramatic had ever happened to her before. I got a little bored with her anxiety, and was saved from being rude to her again by a signal from one of the crew. It was time to embark.

Jute, giving me a last look of sad solidarity, as if I were being left behind, hurried off to join the rest of the crew.

I went back to my beer.

My head was slightly spinning. Newspapers walking or hurrying past me bore notices of murders, serial killers, suicides, sex scandals, ministers entangled in fraud or corruption or vice, children sexually molested by teachers or parents or priests or strangers, or nuclear waste leaking into the world's drinking water and poisoning the rivers, or acid rain devouring nature, of robberies, muggings, assaults on old ladies, or new space missions sent out to investigate distant planets, or racial murderers set free by blind justice, of genocides and perversions, or government cover-ups and dangerous scientific experiments. An endless array of horror stories. It's amazing we don't all go mad with the sheer avalanche of monstrous information that cascades down on us minute by minute. Sometimes it feels as if the planet is in its very last days, as if it is in a terminal spin, with everything screaming of an impending apocalypse. Nightmare stories on the news; nightmare stories wandering around in broad daylight. Our sleep clogged with horrors. Our waking hours crowded with despair. Death, decay, and destruction have taken over the air we breathe. We breathe in death, and breathe out neurosis. We killed off the mysteries in the name of civilisation; we murdered wonder in the crucibles of science – and left the world bare, empty, swimming with barren molecules, inert space, and glorified serial killers.

I felt glum, and my glumness cheered me up. The world isn't as dreadful as all that. It's just that we are shown only the dreadful things. Or maybe the world is even worse. Maybe, late in the morning of humanity, we killed off the secret springs of regeneration, and one by one the magnificent motors of nature are breaking down, leaving us stranded on a planet that will no longer sustain us because we have insulted and abused her too much. Maybe we have filled nature's belly with vile radioactive dinners. Should we be surprised if nature starts to give up the ghost on us?

I got up, finished my drink, and staggered towards the others. Mistletoe was already ahead of me. The world weaved a little. Death wandered everywhere, having light-headed conversations with commuters, travellers, children, their distracted mothers, their pompous fathers, the preening young, the City gents, and the workers. How death conversed with them all, in a fluent cockney accent, or a high-flown accent, or a flat nasal Northern brogue. How death talked, how witty death was, witty to the baby, witty to the old, witty and jocund, talking to all and sundry, like a used-car salesman, or a garrulous taxi-driver. I saw death on the concourse, standing under the clock, looking out at us all, with a kindly smile on his lean face. And if you caught his eye, he nodded like a splendid gentleman with impeccable good manners. And he might sidle up to you and offer you his help.

He'd talk you all the way to your train, or bus, soothing your unease at the beginning of your journey, laughing at your jokes, making a few witticisms of his own in a kindly voice, a few devastating cracks spoken softly, and said almost in passing so that you don't notice them till much later when a lethal thought bubbles up in your head with the question: I wonder what he meant by that?

As we collected our luggage, death came and helped everyone like a friendly porter. Our luggage felt heavier than it had when we left home. (It is always heavier; other invisible luggage have inevitably joined their brothers.) As we begin to set off we look about us and for a moment we see beauty everywhere. The women seem sexier at the beginning of journeys; the men more mysterious. Everyone dreams a little of an incidental romance, of a pleasant adventure, of desirable distraction, of kindly forgetfulness. Travel is a sort of narcotic which you take in through the eyeballs. And death, ever officious, casts a spell over all voyagers, sprinkles us with the enchanted powder of romance, the magic powder of dreaminess, of vanishing vistas, of quaint nostalgia, of dissolving memories. We are leaving our world behind. Things start to recede from us before we begin to move. Our mind says farewell. Every journey is a little dying. Death is the train on which we travel, the bus on which we journey, the car that speeds us there, whether we arrive safely or not. Death is the vehicle of the voyage, but death is never its destination. For, really, if you have drunk as much as I have at the beginning of a journey, you will sense that there are no destinations. Destinations are illusions, merely where the eye comes to a stop, like seeing a wall, an apple, a table, or the face of a loved one. The gaze rests on an object; that is not a destination. A life rests in death; that is not a destination. A destination is different from a destiny.

Seven

As we lumbered towards the train, Jute hurried up to me, slightly breathless, and said:

'I don't trust any of these people. Don't trust any of the crew.'

'Then you are a fool working with us,' I said.

'I'm not including you.'

'I don't want to be excluded. I don't want you to trust me, it bugs my space.'

'You don't really trust the others, do you? I mean, look at them.'

'They seem as disreputable as ever. There's been no change. I'd be worried if Jim had become fantastically successful since the last I saw him. I'd accuse him of sorcery. They are all still a bunch of losers, and that's kind of comfortable.'

'I'm not a loser,' Jute said passionately.

'No, you're a corporate spy.'

'No, I'm not.'

'Oh, yes, you are.'

'You don't like me very much.'

'I'm just being honest about what you are, a spy for the company, spying on us. You're on their side against us, a little brave and incompetent band of outsiders. How can anyone spy on Jim, for God's sake? Don't you have a heart? It's like spying on a tramp, or a baby. Anyway, what do you want? Why are you bugging me, if you get my drift?'

'I'm not bugging you. I just want to talk.'

'You're still worried about your message?'

'Yes.'

'The only time people really want to talk,' I said with malicious insouciance, 'is when they're scared of something. Did the message warn you about death?'

'I don't know if I'm supposed to say.'

'Then don't,' I said casually, knowing it would make her spill. 'Maybe I should.'

Then suddenly I didn't want to know. To know would involve me in her problem. It would become my problem too. I've got enough of my own, thank you, to want to go taking on other people's. Suddenly I felt something contaminating about Jute. She was definitely trying to pass on some of her terrors to me – a famous psychic device used by people all over the world. It works like this: you find someone to offload your deepest troubles and nightmares onto. That way you halve your nightmares and fears while the other person doesn't get a decent night's sleep till the problem is solved. Find enough people and you can keep halving your worries, till you've spread them out thin, and made your life bearable in the process. No, I don't like being in people's confidence. It's like having a dose of radioactive fluid dripped in your ears, or injected into your blood. I hurried away from Jute before she shared her sinister message with me. I hurried and joined the others.

Sam, the cameraman, was talking to Mistletoe about art. Sam was saying something about Vermeer's ability to tantalise without frustrating. Mistletoe spoke about Vermeer's fascination with letters that were being read, secret messages received, about the moment of reading a private missive, the way he makes a private moment oddly public. She reflected on the fact that it was always women who received the letters, reading them alone; as if the paintings were private letters to us meant to be read alone. Then she talked about the mystery of the letters, and how we wonder what they say, and how Vermeer never tells us, leaving us in a state of an unanswered question, in a state of unresolved wonder, the way nature, or life, does.

Sam and Mistletoe had both studied art. Sam used to be a painter and felt he was no good, which he wasn't, in fact he was abominable, and so he had decided to study to be a cameraman instead. He spoke often about wanting to use the camera as a brush, or the screen as a canvas. But, really, all he did was penance, punishing himself as much as possible for his failure to become an artist. And so he had made himself into a sort of stunts man, believing so much that he has to feel the pain if there's to be any value in the work he's doing. He was one of those nut-cases. One of the deluded. If he gets a simple shot, a perfect shot, as a gift of the moment, he distrusts it, and puts himself through incredible contortions to get a mediocre shot, which he values much more than the perfect gift of grace. Well, I think it's a damn inefficient way to work. Or to live. Also, I think it stinks. It's not the suffering that confers the value. If that were the case then we should come close to dying every time we breathe. We should nearly drown every time we drink. The heartbeats would be like hammer blows against our ribcage. The blood would scrape along the canyon of our veins. Walking would be agony. Sex would be excruciating. And going to the toilet would be like trying to expel the Empire State Building. I think the attitude that suffering confers value, confers authenticity, is decidedly suspect. I think it's a neurotic relationship with life, with art, with value. The thing is its own value. And the value of things is always mysterious and enigmatic anyway. Diamond is worth more than water, unless you are dying of thirst. Suffering and martyrdom cannot turn bad art into good art. To my mind, waiting for pain and suffering to confer value is a failure of imagination. And a victory for sentimentality. Some things are easy to look at, but take a lifetime to understand, and they keep changing with your understanding anyway. Some paintings. Some books. Some people. Anyway. Sam is hung up on suffering. I call it his Van Gogh complex, except that Van Gogh is a great artist, and I love his letters, his letters meant for me alone, I mean.

So there is Sam expounding his doctrine of suffering to my Mistletoe, who believes that art ought to be like breathing – breathing not as we breathe habitually, but proper breathing, which has to be re-learned, and practised, almost as a yogic discipline. That is her attitude to art. It ought to be like true breathing, breathing the way God – bless her heart – intended us to breathe, but which we've forgotten. We should create the way nature creates. So you can imagine their conversation. They would agree enthusiastically on most things, and think they were getting along splendidly, and each would think for a moment that they'd found a soul mate, till they would stumble on their central gospels, their artistic credo. Then the awkwardness would set in. Then one would seem like a stranger, suddenly, to the other. Then one would appear an impostor, a fraud. Then estrangement would creep between them, and disillusionment too, and the faint sadness at the loss of an ally, a fellow traveller, that they never had. Then silence would drift between them. Then, afterwards, mild suspicion. And then, forever afterwards, a mild resentment at the other person for not sharing their cherished doctrine, while sharing so much else of their taste in artists and writers, fashion and music. That's what we are most intolerant of: other people who don't share our private central doctrines, the pillars which hold up the secret deficiencies and visible strengths of our lives. Find a person's secret doctrine and you have the key to them, the key to their distress and despair, the key to their self-love.

I gave Sam and Mistletoe another two minutes, predicting to myself the time it would take for her to declare him masochistic in his attitude to art. Meanwhile, we had been walking slowly in the thick crowd alongside the Eurostar train. My mind wandered. And I was beginning to think about the god of journeys when I felt a hand on my shoulder. Someone in the crowd had recognised me from previous documentaries I had foolishly fronted. The horror of recognition passed over me. I scampered away from the greeting that so seduces both the truly famous and the aspirants to fame. I am filled with dread at the easy familiarity which being recognised confers on you; the familiarity and the transparency, and the not knowing what to do with one's face, and not having the right any more to one's private dreams and fantasies. Not having the public freedom to be, the right to one's reveries, one's mind-wanderings, one's easy occupation of space. One now had to properly acknowledge, with graciousness, tact, and forbearance, another human being, a complete stranger, smiling at you with warmth and tentative friendliness. I scampered away. I've seen too many morons quiver with shameless slobbering delight at being recognised. I've seen too many semi-famous idiots whose eyes fairly roam a crowd wondering when they are going to be recognised. I've seen too many who live only for the inanities of fame and I don't want to be in the same bracket of perception. Call it pride. Call it shyness. Call it cussedness. I don't care. But I can't stand the distortion of it all. Besides, till that chap touched me on the shoulder, I was having a perfectly pleasant thought about the god of journeys.

Trying to get back to the thought, which was lost now much as a fish is lost when it wriggles out of your net (too bad, catch another), I heard Propr calling to me. They wanted to take shots of me moving with the crowd. I went over. The shots were quickly set up. I rejoined the crowd. How different everyone became when they knew they were going to be seen, however briefly, by millions. How stiffly some began to walk, how much more animatedly some talked, and even in those that affected disdain or indifference, how studied. That thing they call the camera, it chases away grace, it affects the truth it's supposed to be recording. I wonder if the camera isn't as corrupting as money. The shot passes; sweat gathers on my forehead. Mistletoe comes up to me.

'Been talking to the cameraman,' she says.

'I know.'

'Monstrous attitude to art. Believes good art can only come out of suffering, out of torture. He claims to read only prison literature, the literature of concentration camps, if there is such a thing. And the literature of true-life horror stories, the literature of pain. He's mad.'

'I knew you'd overstate your case.'

'But he's barmy.'

'No, he's not barmy. It's just his own thing. If there's no suffering, there's no art.'

'Someone ought to crush his fingers, then he'd be a genius.'

'Even if you crushed his balls he wouldn't be better than he is.'

'It's not suffering that makes an artist. It's awareness.'

'I know a lot of artists who suffered, and it made their art stink. Still, I suppose he's got a point. Suffering frees some people from their fears, from their mediocrity. For once they can be true. And if they have joy in their souls that joy can be uncaged. They sing for their own consolation, and not for us, an audience. But one ought not to make a principle of it, one way or another.'

'But for him the value of a work changes in relation to how much pain has gone into it.'

'I know. It helps him be better than he might be. He drives himself, he punishes himself, and this makes him work harder...'

'At being worse.'

'Maybe. Actually, yes. He's not the best in the world. But he works hard, and he has a certain naïveté, and he'll do anything for a good shot, which means he is nice to work with if you don't get into a deep conversation with him about art and suffering.'

Jim called me. They needed a different shot. I left the endless crowd. Sam was perched on the edge of a metal fence, upside-down, trying to get a unique angle on the crowd.

I said:

'Why don't you just turn the camera upside-down?'

'Because it would be a different shot,' he replied.

'How?'

'It would look different. It wouldn't have the effort and strain of me hanging upside-down in it.'

'That's mystical nonsense,' I said.

'These things show,' he said. 'They come through.'

Jim wanted me near the front of the train. Propr was taking sound recordings of the crowd murmurings, the platform announcements, the screech of trains grinding on the rails, and, it seemed, the very air itself. Riley ran everywhere Sam went, carrying cases, reloading the camera, and helping him get into contorted positions. Husk bustled about with baggage, and hurried to sort out our seating arrangements and to get good carriages where we could film peacefully. Jute, overcome with a sluggishness more akin to resignation than to laziness, was helping with the movement of the luggage. She had a worried expression on her face, and she kept looking in all directions as if expecting something dreadful at any minute. Mistletoe was already at the door of our compartment, and she was making quick sketches of London's skyline seen from the station, of the tumultuous horde pressing forward to get on the train, of birds in the air, of the pervasive brilliance of a late summer's day, with strong shadows everywhere, and the clear outline of the glinting

61

geodesic dome of transparent glass above us. The long smooth reptilian thread of the blue and yellow train was poised to set off, poised to rush past the countryside, beneath the waters, at wonderful speed designed to postpone time; rushing us away from home, in that mental free-floating state akin to dying, or being born.

Eight

Instead of following the ancient example of the sage who set out alone and travelled under the stars in a state of bliss towards the highest point of the white mountains, there to sit and contemplate the mortal aspects of eternity – I like a fool travelled with a band of fools in the womb of metal at the speed of thoughtlessness towards a reality that poets found it necessary to invent.

The homeless are all there, left behind in the streets and the effacing arches. The dying swell and heave in hospitals and alone in lonely rooms. Those ridden with excruciating diseases and terminal illnesses writhe in courage and terror in private places or in hospital wards or amongst friends and family who look at them with fear in their eyes as they slowly disappear from the world, limb by limb, devoured by an invisible realm that encroaches on this one. The mad swing still in the broken axis of their beings. The troubled in mind can't find a way out of their troubles. Refugees anxiously pace black rooms praying with rosaries or beads for a new hope and a new freedom, while bureaucrats turn their files into endless corridors of cold facts. All over the world famines and wars are in great unholy feasts, gobbling up the bodies of men and women and children, with young babies left to starve, and young men wildly roaming the countryside full of hate, and death growing luxuriantly in fields and breeding in refugee camps. All over the world hatred kindles, death squads fly, dictators execute dissenters, terrorists generate havoc, serial killers buy drinks and chat up innocent women in bars. There are aeroplane disasters, earthquake victims entombed alive beneath indifferent rubble, ships that sink at night, hurricanes and tidal waves that crush the lives of thousands, buses with school children that overturn, and scientists without accountability playing the sinister Frankenstein game, meddling with the matchless mysteries of mortal life. All over the world, presidents are deaf, prime ministers are out of touch, the young stumble towards rude awakenings, the aged stumble towards the long dream of reckonings, those in between are weighed down with the apparent pointlessness of it all. And I, in my heart, where no poison or cynicism ever reaches, I seemingly with a band of fools, who might well be a band of seekers too, I am travelling in disguise towards the place where Hades is averted, turned away, transformed into something else: a hint of paradise lurking in this great universal wound of living.

We never make the journey that we think we are making.

PART TWO

PART TWO

BOOK THREE

BOOK THREE

One

Everyone should have their own windmill, their own thing to tilt at, their own eccentricity. Every member of this crew was odd. They all had a little something wrong in their heads, and it was this little something wrong that brought them together. They were all engenderers of chaos.

When they got on the train, speeding towards the great underwater tunnel, they brought havoc to the first class compartment which they had now established as a base for filming. Jim had managed to sabotage a whole family's peace of mind by getting them to move three times because he needed their table. He managed to alienate all the fellow passengers because he kept pointing at them, saying how odd they looked, and urging Sam to film them all as interesting specimens of stressed humanity. And Sam, in his element, did close-ups of many faces, dashing from one to the other, pointing his camera at couples away on discreet holidays, at businessmen on secret missions, at old ladies who wanted to be left alone, and at families who had an instinctive dislike of the camera's intrusiveness. Jute was herself busy on mysterious trips, tearing up and down the aisle, kicking and bumping into people accidentally. Husk and Riley were rushing around with clapperboards and films, behaving as if the most significant and sacred events were taking place. And Propr kept dangling his furry microphone over people's heads like a white fruit or a Dada exclamation mark, as if he were trying to record their thoughts. Every now and again he would tell people to be quiet, till one of the passengers couldn't stand it any longer and burst into an explosion of expletives, swearing at us for wrecking what he had hoped would be a peaceful journey.

This man was so apoplectic that Jim became fascinated by his rage. Seeing him as an instant metaphor for the stress of the world that had given rise to the Arcadian legend, Jim immediately directed Sam to film the poor man. This made his rage even more towering, and self-destructive. It was wonderful to behold a man so vainly bursting his lungs to illustrate the leaping theme of our journey. For one illuminated moment we all gazed at him, mesmerised, for he was modern man, helpless in his illogical intemperate fury, ranting and lashing out against the universe, tumbling into madness, beyond redemption, powerless, alone, alienated, spinning out of control, less than a man, less than an animal. He raged like that against everything that his exhausted brain could conjure, government taxes, difficult women, asteroids, cancers, ruptured colons, hospital closures, shopping malls, terrorists, absence of private spaces, Loch Ness monsters, child molesters, inconsiderate musicians, pointless television programmes, too much sex everywhere, too many old people; then, abruptly, he sat down, collapsed into a heap, and then shrank, and went on shrinking till he was nearly invisible. The camera stayed on him the whole time till he had exhausted his radioactivity. The camera knew it, and recognised a distant cousin in the radioactive disintegration: the man had been possessed by Hades.

After the possession passed, as after a thunderstorm, the air cleared, and we began to see.

For a moment filming stopped. We sat down to our breakfasts and stared out of the windows silently.

We watched our own lives go past in the shape of the suburban houses, the drab back gardens, the houses that seemed sadder and more monotonous as we sped on.

We were in time's hurtling capsule, death's speeding capsule. Oh, those back gardens, those tilting houses, the lives lived in little paces, such mightiness in potential in such small places. Such drabness, such sameness. We sped past them all, past the back view of our lives. The way it seems to strangers, never to us. What have we settled for, under this glorious sun? How did our lives lose so much colour, so much outline? The back view of suburban houses is the very mirror of our receding soul: of Hades advancing, of time shrinking, of death anonymising.

Two

First there was Eden, then the Fall; then the Golden Age, then the descending eras of Silver, Bronze and Tin; and then there was Arcadia.

Arcadia is our secular Eden. It is both a real place in the Peloponnese and an imaginary place. In legend, it is the birthplace of Hermes. It was first dreamed up by Theocritus, but made more famous by Virgil. In Virgil's hand Arcadia became an imaginary landscape of lovers and shepherds, a pastoral realm, a place of strangely disordered passions, faintly presided over by the absent shadow of the great god Pan. A place of dreaming, and songs, an oasis, a refuge from the corrupting cities, a semi-ideal landscape, a qualified paradise. A place with the quietly troubling presence of death, and exile, and stony mountains, and suicide, and sinister shadows, a place that cannot be dwelt in for ever. Then, with the passing of centuries, something happened to Virgil's Arcadia. It became transformed into a terrain of the mind, a terrestrial paradise, a place of tranquillity and rural calm, the domain of the yearning spirit.

Arcadia is a dream of city-dwellers, of people exiled from nature. In the old days, everyone had access to a bit of nature. Peasants worked the fields, and lived and suffered within nature's cycles. In the days before the mass deforestation of the earth, even city-dwellers found themselves surrounded by woods. From the lowly peasant to the king, all had access to nature, to the cyclicity of things, to the reminder of something greater than themselves. Now nature is more and more absent. Eden has shrunk to a city back garden. But the little garden, the town park, reminds us of what we have lost. And they connect us to the quiet vastness of the lost thing much as a lake reminds us of the sea. It keeps the dreaming alive.

Arcadia is always elsewhere. For Virgil and the Romans, it was in Greece. For us now, it is a vision of the countryside, of hills, dells, meadows, valleys, brooks. The great god Pan is not dead. The great god Pan is refracted, but forgotten. Our modern neurosis is Pan's revenge. Our craving for nature is our craving for reunion with the sublime, for oneness, for rejuvenation.

Three

Suburbia sped past, shabby under the brilliant August sun. Towns, fields, little churches, cricket greens, shopping centres with imitation brick structures. Back gardens, patches of dry green, like contemplating the ocean in an empty bucket. Dreariness. Pallidness. People sunning themselves and staring dreamily at the hurtling train, staring and thinking of journeys to faraway places, of adventures. (Or just what a menace trains are to their lives.) When the train speeds past, and disappears, a little of the light of dreaming goes out in your eyes. Perhaps that is why all over the world people wave at trains, wave at the people on trains. Perhaps they are waving at dreams of escape, of a better life, of freedom. We, voyagers on trains, carry their aspirations with us. We have become glamorised, touched with grace. We become instant metaphors of life's journey, arcing from past to present to future. When they wave they are saying: take a little of me with you wherever you are going, on your adventures, and don't forget those of us at home, tending the gardens, guarding the home fires...

Golden sunshine all around. Shadows solid in fast glimpses. Arcadia is a place of strong sunlight and strong shadow. Where there is illumination there must also be solid shadows, patches of mystic darkness.

The train meandered through open countryside that received the golden light gratefully. Such gold is rare in lands that know long winters. And with wondrous radiance, it makes the land swim in something akin to worship. The gold in the sky is like the appearance of a benign god, spreading benedictions all through the land, deep into its next harvest. On days like this happiness becomes visible.

Four

Intuitions in the Dark (1)

Imagine the shimmer of sunlight on bright things and the approaching tunnels. Consider the swift movement from light to darkness. All tunnels have strange effects on the minds of people. The vistas of the world disappear, and the world surrenders to an omnipotent darkness. Such a tight space, such vast implications of darkness. The mind contracts. The spirit folds inwards. An open sky gives way to a closed world. And for a moment a hush descends on the travellers. Night has come upon everyone. A brief night of the mind as of the eyes. A frisson of incomprehension. A hint that the world is not all we see, that the world is an invention of our senses. A flash of the mind unmoored, afloat, in a dark space. When the light of the world goes out, the mind, briefly, goes out too. And then there is a swift return to a primeval condition, when darkness was a god, a god as revered and as strong as the god of light. But light can be manufactured. Darkness, technologically, has not been manufactured. In society, the opposite is true: it is easier to make darkness than it is to create light.

Five

Intuitions in the Dark (2)

Tunnels give way to open spaces. The spirit widens, experiences sudden liberation. The spirit contracts again when we enter another tunnel. The dark becomes less terrifying, the open spaces less liberating. But when we emerge through darkness into open countryside, and see people walking, or playing in fields, or sauntering along with their restless dogs, we look at them more warmly, more intensely; we fix our eyes on them, and stare without judgement or opinion any more. For a moment, we see purely, and let the world speak to us in a language deeper than words, a language of the sea-bed of humanity, from the place where the gods used to whisper to us about our essential nature. Then, for a moment, the inscriptions are everywhere, and all reality becomes pure inscriptions without words.

And then comes another tunnel, and an inward seeing. The shock of being thrown on that inward darkness which reveals an inward light. Memories, faces, scraps of thought, fractions of intuitions, hints of the future, race past in the mind's inward space. The tunnel makes us see inward, against our will. An open-eyed dreaming ensues. Thoughts become stiller; thoughts experienced in no language, but in the material of consciousness, sweeter for being in this *prima materia* of the spirit, the original currency of the mind, the elastic, intangible language of air.

Tunnels make you think things. If you were asked to define them, you simply would. There would be no 'abouts', no subjects. Just pure thinking in the light of the inward dark.

Six

Intuitions in the Dark (3)

Then another exposure to the world. Fields and factories and trees and flowers and the distant vistas and churchyards and graveyards all crooked and children playing football. And a smile raised to the face as the mind bubbles up from deep down to the open sky of consciousness. A gentle soaring, a changed gear of thought, from solitude to the communality of the eyes, from a private world to a shared world, from solitude to sunniness. The feeling of sunlight warming the eyeballs. The gaze resting on the daisies and the oak trees. When the announcement sounds, crackling over the loudspeakers, telling us of our approach to the grand tunnel that takes us under water, where we will travel at great speed for twenty minutes, the spirit changes, the smile freezes, the mind prepares for immersion, for dislocation, for paradox. The mind goes into one of its finer acts of denial. It pretends not to think of death when in fact that is precisely, indirectly, what, deep down, it is thinking about and preparing for, even when it is aware that it is perfectly safe...

Seven

Intuitions in the Dark (4)

Unreality dislocates the body, sends the mind into contortions. A tunnel is a mental event; a technological creation of a primal condition. A tunnel is a dark spiritual event, a manageable crisis, a reinvention of the caves which nature creates in mountains, under water, beneath rocks. Civilisations go through tunnels. Eras go through them. Cultures go though them. The darkness unfurls questions about reality. Outer and inner become blurred. And philosophy is born.

In tunnels the mind undergoes a little initiation. All initiations into the mysteries of life take place in dark spaces. The Orphic rituals were enacted in caves. The ancient Egyptians held their rites and rituals of rebirth in dark tombs in pyramids. Self undertakes its rituals of differentiation, of individuation, in darkness, in crisis. In tunnels we rehearse dying. Tunnels are a little death, a death with the senses wide awake, an open-eyed borderline between dying and living. In this state first principles spring on to the stage of the spirit, certainties dissolve, fears surface, anxieties multiply, and questions float everywhere like sinister fishes in the calm under water of the mind. How much more so when the tunnel is under water, when disaster can strike at the slightest breach of technology's great walls?

Eight

Intuitions in the Dark (5)

Going underground, in a tunnel, through darkness, is different to being in the air, above the ground. In the latter, you are above the world, rehearsing death in its soaring phase, freedom aflight, surveying the kingdom of things, of the terrestrial realm, among the clouds. Above, the mind drifts with notions of angels, of the heavens, of weightlessness. But in the former, you are in the earth, below the surface, encompassed by matter, floating through the womb of beginnings, for birth begins in darkness, the first and most momentous journey of them all, or the last. Or the place of destiny.

For the womb is as much destiny as chamber. The womb contains it all, inner light, first formations, rehearsal of all the future stages. The womb is the microcosm of the world. It is the primal stage, the first drama, the original theatre. We are delivered from the inner womb to the outer womb. The world is a giant womb too, in which, maybe, we rehearse being born, rehearse our futures, prepare our ends.

The world is as much a destiny as the womb is, surrounded by sky and air, water and fire and matter. And all of humanity is but one being, one multiple child, one cell, one idea, one thought, one drama, enclosed within a stage.

And the ether beyond the sun, the universe at large, has its greater darkness, encompassing, much as the womb does.

And speeding in a train, within a tunnel, is much like a movable pod or womb, a journey through death as towards light. But it is the death aspect that is the most enlightening. For how we are in that movable dying tells us how we will be in the light of the life to come. The tunnel gives meaning and value to the light, if we get there...

And it was in the tunnel, in the dark stage of an unscripted initiation, that the unfolding drama of the muddling crew revealed its next act.

Nine

Darkness loves mischief, and forces out revelation. And as filming was temporarily halted because of the tunnel, and as the crew hung around, performing their time-filling acts, the darkness pounced on Jute and loosened her fear. Suddenly, she began to scream. And what she was screaming about seemed to have something to do with the peculiar message she had received at the beginning of the journey.

'My death is so unimportant,' she cried. 'Who cares about anybody's death anyway?'

Jim hurried over to her. She was chewing her handkerchief. Her cheekbones were accentuated by the alternating darkness and light of the tunnel.

'What's the matter?' Jim asked.

'I just saw Malasso, and he was trying to kill me.'

'Have you seen him before?'

'No.'

'Then how do you know it was him?'

'Just a feeling I had. A creepy, evil feeling.'

'But it could have been anybody.'

'It was him all right.'

'How can you be so sure?'

'I am. It was him. He looked evil, and he was trying to kill me.'

'But why?'

'Because I've got the map.'

'What map?'

'You'd like to know, wouldn't you?'

'Yes, what map?'

'Can't tell you, or he'll try and kill you too.'

'You're making this up, Jute.'

'Believe what you like, my death is so unimportant anyway.'

'Stop saying that.'

'It's true though.'

'No, it's not, and you know it.'

'It's true,' said Jute, softening.

'Where did you see him?'

'Who?'

'The man you said was trying to kill you.'

'Here, right in front of me, in the darkness.'

'And how did he try to kill you?'

'With a knife.'

'A knife?'

'Yes, a short knife.'

'Did he say anything?'

'Only what he'd said before.'

'When?'

'In the message.'

'What message?'

'The message I got, the red one.'

'Oh, that one. What did it say? You never told us.'

'Can't tell you.'

'Why not?'

'All I can say is that it's not terribly important if I die. Or you. Or you,' she said, pointing at each one of us in turn with her long crooked vengeful finger.

Then she fell silent, as we thundered through the darkness of the tunnel...

Ten

When Jim got back to his seat he was surprised to find an envelope on the table, with his name neatly typed on it. He looked all around him in the dim light of the carriage. All the other crew members were either busy at one thing or another, or snatching a brief sleep before the frenzy of filming was resumed.

The envelope was white, his name typed in black. When he opened it, looking about him all the time, he found nothing inside but a set of instructions concerning the next stage of the journey. He breathed a deep sigh of relief. He had been beginning to believe that there was truth in the hysterical cries of two of his crew members claiming that they had received messages hinting at dreadful things, messages seemingly delivered from thin air.

When he came to think of it, even the materialisation of these instructions was a puzzle. There was something sinister about it. He had been made to understand that information would be given to him before the next stage of the journey. He had expected this to take place at the hotel in Paris. But to find that the next stage was in the middle of the tunnel, with information planted in the confusion following a general darkness, troubled him. All his fellow passengers suddenly appeared sinister.

Jim got up and, weaving with the motion of the train, went to ask the other crew members if they had seen anyone place the envelope on his table, or whether they had anything to do with it themselves. They were as puzzled as he was, and began to believe that Jute had indeed seen Malasso in the darkness.

The only problem was that no one knew what he looked like, and no one knew if he even really existed. He was merely a rumour that had become a reality, an elusive reality. And they all sat together, trying to understand the nature of the mystery they were faced with.

The new instructions were simple enough. At the end of this train journey they were to approach the train driver and conduct an interview with him at his house in the suburbs of Paris. Before then they might be joined by someone from the organisation whom they wouldn't notice, and if they did they were to ignore him. After the interview they were to converge at a certain point outside the Louvre, where they would be provided with a map and directed to the next interview, the process having already been arranged for them.

The crew would get its Arcadian interviews, but Malasso would get what he wanted. For the first time, Jim sensed their journey was an arcane voyage, the interviews and places forming an inner script, a sacred script even. He felt that they were all unwitting parts of a sublime riddle, a mystical conundrum, a travelling cryptograph. Back at his table, he tried to work out, by alphabet, a name or map or hint of what their journey secretly represented. But he couldn't find any order to it, couldn't find any visible clues, and he was baffled by the apparent inconsequentiality of it all.

Eleven

The other crew members, however, were enjoying a brief rest in the tunnel. Their heads were drooping. They had no feeling for conundrums or cryptographs. They were mostly plain souls, with a touch of cynicism here, and a flash of scepticism there. They were mostly people who took life as they found it, and were unwilling to probe too deeply into what they couldn't fathom. They were people of appearances, people of the senses, of the skin, of the surface.

They were people of appearances, except for the couple who sat staring into the darkness, the drunken presenter and his painter companion. They cultivated wakefulness. Irony was his favoured beverage. Wisdom was the great secret food of his spirit. Caustic vision was the deceptive mode in which he functioned in the world, preferring to be seen as a wild and bitter man than as a lovable clown or a forgivable fool, the other two disguises open to a man of spirit and intelligence in an age without a centre, an age without beliefs, an age of emptiness. He hid his wisdom, his genius for living, and his mighty love beneath what appeared to be a coruscating madness. This effort cost him dear, for the mask often became the face, became the visage by which the world recognised him. He became like an actor who played his part on stage longer than he lived his truth in life. His role sometimes overwhelmed his reality.

His father had named him Lao. It was a name he had hated as

a child, because it was so alien, but which he had come to like as an adult, because it was intangible.

Lao sat there, staring past his companion, into the darkness. Having overheard the latest drama with the envelope, and watched the baffled reaction of the crew, he noted how silent Jute had become, and how solemn Jim now was, as he contemplated the envelope and its instructions. Jim had not come to Lao, discouraged by his forbidding and apparent cynicism, his verbal cruelty, and his permanent air of non-involvement. This air was one of his best cloaks, a garment of invisibility. It enabled him to see everything, without being seen, to hear everything, without being heard. It gave him the space for vast inner and outer freedoms.

Twelve

Jute sat impassively, staring but not seeing, thinking about all the messages she had received in her life, and not being able to remember any of them. She felt, suddenly, sitting there, as if she had been, all her days, missing out on secret and valuable things. Her mother had died when she was a little girl and all her life she had grown with two warring convictions in her mind, the finality of death, and the impermanence of death. Which is to say that she believed that when someone dies nothing of them remains, they went to nowhere land, they vanished completely, devoured or erased by the gods of the vacuum. Not even memory keeps them alive, because, eventually, memory too dies. On the other hand she was convinced that the dead are still here, somewhere, in spirit. She dreamed often about her mother, and in these dreams her mother told her useful things, prepared her for events to come. And Jute knew for certain that her mother whispered messages to her all through the years, warning her here, guiding her there. These were not loud voices that would cause alarm, but faint wind-whispers, things heard and not heard, heard almost through the agency of her own private thoughts, so that it was almost impossible to distinguish between her own thoughts and the whispers.

And so Jute saw the world dually. She never admitted to the latter view, the wind-whispers. As a faithful company woman she never for a moment slackened on the dour materialism expected of her. In all conversations to do with higher phenomena she affected complete scepticism, even scorn for all those who suggested that there might be more to life than met the eye. She loudly affected to prefer what could be seen and demonstrated, 'real life' as she put it, to any fancy notions of beings, life beyond death, intangibles, the miraculous, invisibles. And so she too lived a role. And the role overwhelmed her reality. She went days and weeks without the whispers of her mother – the most awful days of her life. And the anguish of it made her more miserable than anything the world did to her. And she had to think her way back to her true secret beliefs, to open herself privately to what she knew in the core of her being, before she could begin to dream of her mother again, and of her childhood, when she had been so happy, as if she had lived in an enchanted garden. To dream and wander about with those feathery whispers, those friendly words and that breezy laughter filling her with reassurance and a cheerfulness which she concealed beneath a grim and dour exterior.

But now, sitting alone, her mind empty, she tried to summon her mother. Ever since she first heard about the journey she had stopped seeing her mother, stopped hearing her, and dreaming about her. Jute was in the middle of her own wasteland. There was no love in her life. She was in a desert without an oasis. For two months now her spirit had been barren. She had lived so much in scepticism, had affected so much disdain for the notion of Arcadia on which they were now embarked, had suppressed her openness, had professed too much her dislike of airy-fairy notions, that she had drifted, without knowing when, into a dark and complex place, a tangled place. Her sleep had never been so troubled. Monsters and men with knives, whispering murder and abduction, appeared to her more frequently. Since she received the message in Husk's flat, her life had been in a turmoil that she dared not admit to anybody. There was a mighty revolt in the palaces within her. There was insurrection in the land. Her sleep had gone to pieces; and the only voices she heard were harsh ones, and her only dreams took the shapes of the idealisation of the message, took nasty forms, and plagued her. Malasso became a constant visitor in her nightmares. He seemed everywhere, the incarnation of an evil she couldn't deny was also part of her. How often did she see herself being murdered, raped, pursued, hounded, tied up, brutalised, mocked, laughed at, and isolated in her dreams? How often had she waited, lingering, for the sea-breeze voice of her mother? Jute sat now and stared. Nothing was coming through to her. She saw nothing, distorted everything, and was alone in her darkness, suspicious and disintegrating, and too proud to admit it.

Thirteen

The announcement woke up the travellers. The tunnel was coming to an end. They had emerged from the sea-depths. Beverages were still available at the bar...

The crew stirred. Jim, scratching his balding head, awoke from his wakeful slumber, from his cumbrous pondering of the envelope and his next set of instructions. Riley was polishing the lens of her beloved camera. Sam, eyes arrowed, was pursuing the angles of his next shot, thinking of faces, flowers, children, heights, helicopter flights, upside-down visions, penitential prospects, existentialism. Husk, always aflutter with activity, had begun a hundred things, arranging teas, phoning ahead, fixing interviews, studying her instructions with pursed lips and an unfriendly expression on her oddly judgmental face. Propr, bewhiskered, gnarled, and twisty like an Egyptian rope, or a thin wind-blown oak, with his glasses always magnifying his eyes, and his moustache conferring on him a comical expression faintly reminiscent of silent movie clowns, Propr sat there, drowsy, but always listening. Propr was the finely tuned ear of the world. Everything for him was a sound. He was a poor listener to conversation, but an intense listener to the world's noises and susurrations. The finer noises fascinated him most. The least heard, the keener his engagement. He had partially retired, having worked in the same line of business for more than thirty years. And he had only accepted this job when it was explained to him that Arcadia had something to do with goats and sheep and shepherds. He tended a farm up in the Celtic inlands, listening to the lowing of cows, and the piping of all variety of birds whose names and sounds he knew by heart and could match at a moment's notice.

But he too was going through dislocating times. Trouble raged in his land. Inheritance problems, a wife that ran off with a neighbour, a death in the family, a daughter that fled from home swearing never to return, financial worries. Propr hadn't known peace for almost a year now, but couldn't admit it even to himself. And so he lost himself in listening, in delving into the noises and sounds of the world. He submerged himself in their subtleties and intensities. In that world of sounds nothing mattered, everything was pure, and the fact that his life was falling apart, that his farm was being repossessed, was a fiction that danced like an imp on the edges of his mind, where other fictions, like capricious goats, are allowed to play harmlessly...

Fourteen

And then there was Mistletoe, silent, submerged, and waiting. A life begun in happiness, a childhood rich in variety and freedom, much early travel, much of the world seen and loved. Then a life that took a wrong turning, and the right road regained later than she would have wished. Blessed with an ease of spirit that falls so easily into a love of rebellion. She was one of the intelligent ones who have to be lazy in order to be awoken by failure. The early recklessness. The ambiguous blessings of beauty, feline grace, and deep-scented sensuality. The early reliance on easy talent. Then being too favoured and lucky. Then unfavoured and unlucky. Then misused by men. Then disillusioned and disenchanted. Talents not developed early, lost on the way, wandering, beautiful, optimistic still, and lost. Wreckages of past dreams about her. Then despair and loss of faith in life. Then drink and drugs and hopelessness and believing in everything, believing in nothing. Emptiness. Lovelessness. And then touched by good fortune which never really deserted her. Finding new friends. Finding a friend in Lao. Then the slow journey back, through art, to sanity. Meanwhile, what a ring of connections. Disowned by parents, cut off from homeland, almost friendless, heart dry but for the pulses of new friendships and the quickening of art. Her sensuality fabulous, her body suspicious of love. Her eyes suspicious, in spite of a capacity for abundant warmth and great love. A heart frozen, a mind awake. Waiting for life's thaw, clinging on to friendship, silent, submerged, like a submarine, an iceberg, magisterial...

Fifteen

And then with a blasting of a whistle, long and piercing like a weird sea-animal waking from an agonising hibernation, with a noise of grinding metal, and a howl heard from the rails, and a rattling and a scattering, the train thundered out of the tunnel into the gorgeous light of the French countryside. And all hearts quickened. Motion, voices, laughter. Solitudes were broken. And the wonder of seeing the world again, its fields, its flowers and trees, its varied colours of green and yellow, blue and orange, the clear heavens, the rich sunshine pouring on the expanse of turquoise and gold, the converging sky and land, the spaces of light in which the eye can roam. As if creation had been restored.

And a sense of magic stirrings beginning somewhere within. A quickening of recognition, a sense of place, an expectation, an attitude of romance, an inclination to *joie de vivre*, a freedom, a hope of escape, the breeze of a new unconfinement. Youthfulness, bohemianism, the secret desire to be an artist, or at least to be artistic, the self unloosed in a different language, associations with beauty, charming eccentricity, with wine and mellow drunkenness, with a land of art, where artists used to converge from all over the world as at an Arcadia in a darkening age, a place where freedoms meet, and art flowers in a thousand varied colours and forms, where outrage is stylised, where poetry is favoured over prose, elegance over energy, where the faun wakes in the long afternoon, and corruption seethes but never paralyses, where revolt simmers, and the ghosts of history wander the air speaking in paradoxes, a place imagined, more true in the mind than on earth.

A rich tapestry of sensations awoke as the voyagers sped over bridges, through orchards, across fields with golden haystacks.

Sixteen

The crew meanwhile leapt into action. Filming was resumed. All private troubles were sublimated into work's necessity. Jute had forgotten her anguish, Jim his anxiety, Husk her paranoia, Propr his cuckoldry, Sam his impending divorce, Riley her paralysing fear of death. All except Lao, who sat still in his seat, looking out over the fields of green and gold. His mind wandered between a cynical perception of everything to an enchanted vision of all things, between loathing and loving, malice and magic, between the mask of the heart and the nakedness of the heart. He looked at Mistletoe. She was serenely sketching, lost in her kingdom. He said:

'Isn't it strange how most significant human activity has to do with loss? Because we lose things we try to find them. The trying sends us on a journey. We encounter other things, things we hadn't noticed that we had lost: and then we create. Art springs out of both alienation and loss. Art replaces what we have lost in spirit. It is therefore a magic replacement. And so it is with Arcadia, it seems to me. We've long lost our easy relationship with nature, with the universe. And so the ancient Romans betrayed themselves as the first alienists when they dreamt up and crafted the legend of Arcadia. It showed just how fucked up they were that they needed to invent an ambiguous Eden for themselves, where love is akin to madness. And so it would seem that art is a condition of unease, of dislocation, of being out of it all, an exile. Art cannot come from the happy and contented, from the lucky and the beautiful, from the blessed and the whole, unless an unrevealed tragic condition or premonition dwells under it all like an unseen volcano or an unsuspected cataclysm about to wipe away all that unnatural tranquillity. The last days of beautiful things are the most artistic. It seems then that art is a secret sign of dwelling under a guillotine, under a swinging sign of doom, under a hidden question mark, beneath the dread of death, in unwholeness, wanting to be healed and to heal, with a whiff of mortality and the inferno in one's spirit, with a sense of sin, of unredemption. It seems that art is a magic plea, a magic howl, an enchanted cry, a delaying of madness, a deflection of insomnia, a canalising of negative energies. Art is finding one's way in the dark, seeing with one's fingers, divining water in the desert, creating an abstract realm made up in the mind of others to replace the realms of childhood and innocence lost for ever with the death of a mother. Art is finding a new homeland, and yet always setting sail. It is being deceived and lured by the gods into roaming the whole wide earth many times over and leaving bright cities behind in search of that which can never be found, but which seems as if it might be found, because of a dream which keeps moving like a bird, a magic bird, or a love, or a dream of rest, or the hint of a beautiful city in the middle of an ocean. But it keeps driving us on, keeps us going, till the skeleton wanders into a golden gate, and into a sunlit landscape where the sunlight is a perpetual darkness, while another part of us has ceased its wanderings, having found what it was looking for in a place where nothing is ever lost or found, a place without a name or an idea. Which is why there is a fatality in finding, and an agony in seeking. But between seeking and finding there is another place, a special place, and maybe it is such a place that we journey towards now, that we call Arcadia, a place that for some is a book, a piece of music, a face, a photograph, a landscape, a lover, a city, a house, a land, a ritual, a path, a way of being, even. Maybe, my dear friend, we are journeying towards an elusive thing in the desert, where thirst is quenched miraculously in the air, and the fragrance of a great love lingers in the shade...'

Seventeen

Mistletoe looked up at him from her drawing. She looked at him for a long time, as if his features had altered somewhat. Then, returning to her sketching, and thereby creating an air of significance, she said:

'You should write that down.'

'I'm only interested in writing down things I can't say.'

'You're perverse.'

'That's what the crab said to the horse.'

'What?'

'You're perverse, why don't you walk sideways, like me?'

'And what did the horse say?'

'The horse was too polite to say anything, and trotted off. But the story has a sequel.'

'What is it?'

'When the horse was out of sight of the crab, it stopped and wondered why it didn't run sideways like the crab. The horse had often secretly admired this ability in the crustacean. And so the horse, making sure that no one was around to witness its folly, practised trotting sideways. The horse found it very difficult at first, then increasingly pleasurable, and refreshingly novel. Over the next few weeks the horse kept up this practice till it mastered the art of running sideways as much as it was possible for a horse to do. And then came the day of the great games and festivities of the horses. And in the games the horse astounded all the other horses with its elusive capacity, its ability to escape capture by being able, very swiftly, to run sideways, to change direction effortlessly and without thinking about it. And so it became the most accomplished and mysterious horse among all the horses. Many years later, when it had long been acclaimed as the greatest of all the horses, after it had become a legend in its own horse-time, when this great horse was dying, its children gathered round and asked the secret of its longevity, success, and enormous influence. The horse said: "I befriended all the large and little creatures, and learned from them. In one word, I seemed perverse." The children laughed and were amazed. And when the great horse asked why they were amazed the children said: "We met the greatest and most fascinating crab, profoundly revered by its people and many others. And when we asked the secret of its great life the crab said more or less the same thing as you." The great horse smiled and said: "Then it must be the only crab that knows how to run straight as well as sideways, and also how to gallop. What we sometimes call perversity, my children, is really genius at work." "And what is genius, father?" the children asked. "Common sense raised to the highest," the old horse replied. And then he expired. That is the end of my improvisation.'

Eighteen

Mistletoe stared at him again. Then she resumed drawing, and was silent for a while. They listened to the train's whistle, as they shot past the golden countryside. Then Mistletoe, in a gentle voice, said:

'You really ought to write that down too. Shame to just waste it on me.'

And Lao, as if anticipating her remark, said:

'I waste good things that I might find excellent things. Don't you think we should try and go beyond ourselves?'

'Yes, but only if we have made good use of what we've been given.'

'Nature is spendthrift. Look at the trees in autumn, shedding all those leaves. Look at the way plants and trees and flowers scatter their pollen on the wind, not caring where it goes...'

'But trusting that a few of those seeds will fall on good soil, and grow.'

'But such generosity, Mistletoe, such hurling out of so many millions of seeds so that only one or two will grow. What extravagance! And yet see how nature remains, see how abundant, how winter bares her of leaves, makes her stark, how she doesn't complain or fight or apologise or panic. But she grows inwardly, gathering in silence and in secret all the sap for the new season. She prepares meticulously, within the castle of her bark. Nature knows no defeat. Trees and plants are not conquered by winter. They wait. They prepare. They work with winter. They work round winter. They probably like winter. They probably need winter's victory. It gives them time to prepare the next stage of their growth and evolution. In the same way the generosity of trees is not foolishness, or folly, or indiscrimination, but greatness, nature's highest economy. Maybe the vast production of seeds is a fabulous inner incentive for growth, for greater outward reach and deeper grip on the earth. Maybe trees are more powerfully motivated and become more awesome, more durable, because they produce so much seed. After all, it wouldn't need so much nourishment and become so much if it merely produced the exact number of seeds or pollen required to propagate the next generation. If this number was say ten or twenty, then the whole tree might not do such deep work inside itself, such great thickening of its trunk, such profound exploration with its roots, such vast spanning with its branches, such upward reach. You can't have greatness without abundance.'

'But,' said Mistletoe, 'trees are not great because they produce such vast number of seeds or pollen. Otherwise, when they no longer...'

'Oak trees, thousands of years old, still produce seeds: nature is always generative, always productive. There can be no greatness without productivity, of one kind or another.'

'But for some that greatness is producing pollen, for others shade. For some it is sheer endurance...'

'The last resort of the mediocre...'

'...for others it is sheer concentration. Titian had genius and endurance. Raphael had genius and concentration.'

'But they are both productive. Titian produced a lot. Raphael continues to inspire production, and so he produces through others, through time, much like Mozart.'

'So you agree then that there are different kinds of generosity. There's the generosity of pouring out plenty of potentialities; and there's the generosity of having vast potentialities in the few things given out. One is quantity, the other quality.'

'You've moved to the other side of the argument. You're now on my side.'

'No, I'm not.'

'Yes, you are.'

'I'm not.'

'I pour out what's at the top to get to what's at the bottom. I'm interested only in the essentials, the most intangible things. To find them I have to get rid of so much dross, so much fine rubbish, so much froth. I have to get rid of all my thoughts, opinions, perceptions. They are not important, and can be had by anybody, or will be, or variations of them can occur to anybody. No, Mistle, I'm not interested in me. I'm interested in what's not me that's within me. I'm interested in getting to the things in me that're beyond me, beyond speech, but which can be refracted in words, or channelled through words, or like light be made at least to illuminate a room or house or world through the transparency of the windows, or the lovely coloured glass of art. I get rid of so much of myself in order to let the light come through.'

'You can do that more economically.'

'How?'

'Through silence.'

Nineteen

Lao was jolted by that word – silence. It seemed to open up to him, in a landscape-flash, briefly, what his journey was truly about. The word knocked out something in his mind; and in a perfect stillness, which he had been unaccustomed to for a long time, he gazed into a warm and lighted inner realm as his eyes looked out into a brilliantly lit landscape of rocks, flowers, distant churches, high roads, and barley fields. His mind was in a place of sweetness unknown to him. From every pore, without knowing how, he drank in the lovely liquid of that state. He had a half-cynical smile on his face, the kind of smile that doubters have when they are being inwardly stirred, inwardly touched by the very thing they doubt. It was a smile both of resistance and submission, of denial and delight, of the spirit knowing a thing to be true and of the head still refusing to accept it as true.

'Even if we don't believe in it, we need the Arcadian dream,' Lao said suddenly. 'If only as a place where the spirit can rest. In life the body can have many holidays, but the spirit has so few. The body's holidays are simple: sex, sun, beach, sea, sleep. But the spirit's holidays are rarer: they are ideas, inspiration, Arcadias. The holidays of the spirit are more important than those of the body. The body has lots of holidays while it's alive, and a long one when dead. The spirit has few holidays when in life. The holiday of the spirit replenishes civilisations, makes spiritual evolution effortless, and makes it possible for us to go up to the higher levels that we despair of reaching. Holidays of the spirit help us assimilate faster and more thoroughly all that we are and have been, they help the inner distillation, and they make us grow faster, greater and more organically. Holidays of the spirit are what bring about our true transformation from chrysalis to butterfly, from weakness to wisdom, from saplinghood to strength. We need Arcadia, for without it we will die of our neuroses.'

Then suddenly Lao stood up and went in search of Jim, for he had been faintly touched, in his core, for the first time, by the mysterious nature of what he had thought was a truly bad idea for a televised journey.

Twenty

But when he found Jim he encountered not a director in control, but one falling out of control. Not a man at ease, but a man ill at ease. A man disintegrating, collapsing, staring into an abyss, into his final failure. Jim was in a deep funk, a stinking malaise, with his eyes large and unfocused, as if he had already surrendered his soul to the sweet god of despair. Lao found a man who was all but finished. Jim didn't move when Lao touched him on the shoulder. A dead zone surrounded him. Lao sat down opposite Jim, and stared out of the window. He gazed at the tapestry of the passing world. Only the deep can talk to the deep. The deep calls forth the deep. Only those who know deep despair can talk to the deeply despairing. Lao said:

'Let me tell you the secret of the butterfly.'

But before he could begin, Jim looked out of the window, as if he were contemplating jumping. Then he turned his mournful woebegone face back towards Lao, ran his fingers through the few scattered tufts of white hair he had left and, in the gloomiest voice, said:

'It's all falling apart, old boy. I can't cope. I'm a mess. I'm a scarecrow, except not even the crows are scared any more. It's all falling to pieces. My hair is falling out in clumps. It's embarrassing. The stuffing is coming out of me. The weave is coming undone. The straw is falling off my head, sticking out of my ears, old boy. If it weren't so abject it would be comic. I can say this to you because you're a mess too, but you're an artistic mess, and in a strange way you hang together. I can talk to you because you're authentic and wouldn't give me any bullshit about things being all right and the human spirit can overcome and stuff like that, stuff that makes a man want to cut his throat because he simply can't find it in him to overcome and be so damned positive. I'm swimming in failure. I'm drowning in the stuff. I'm fucked. No redemption or atonement for me. I'm the bathwater that God threw out. Failure behind me, failure in front of me, failure all the way up to my eyeballs. I stink of the stuff. All my life I've let everyone down. My kids can't look up to me and have taken to joking about what a bad film-maker I am. Made the worst films in history. Got the vote for it twice. Twice voted the worst film maker of the year. When did I last make a film anyway? You must have been in nappies then. I tell you, Lao, someone has set me up, they've set me up for the final fall. They've stitched me up. This is curtains, I can smell it. The last act in a non-career. Began by being bad and died at his worst. The best thing that can happen is if I die on this journey, mid filming. That way there's no last act, no last film, only mid-film. Then you guys can carry on, make the film to the end, make it to the best of your ability, and if it's any good they'll say that Jim inspired an inspired movie at the end. They'll speak of my magnificent swan song. I'll be redeemed. That's my Arcadia, if you really want to know. To make one good film. To die in the odour of excellence. A great last act. Something for the chaps in the back seats. A good man comes through at the last. Never write a man off till you've heard his last song. His life was crap, but at the end he was inspired. My father didn't manage it. Lived in failure, died in failure. Not a shred of excellence anywhere. Wasn't even mediocre. He distrusted, he loathed excellence. A walking failure. He made failure into a mythology. Then he sold us on it. Haven't been able to shake his shadow since. Haven't even been able to react against him. It would be too much like betrayal. And to betray his failure would be the ultimate, it would be to judge the poor sod. I never stood a chance. Never got a foot in. Why are you all on this journey with me anyway? I'm a mess. I inspire no confidence. You guys and ladies are great; it's me that's all wrong, I'm the fraud, can't you smell it? There are things going on in this journey that I don't understand. Why me? Why flog a dead horse? Why humiliate the humiliated? Why saddle me with such a film concept when everyone knows I don't stand a chance in hell of delivering? They knew I'd make a mess of it, so why did they choose me? Is this a company joke? I tell you, I'm the least equipped person to make a journey to Arcadia, to notions of earthly paradise. I'm better equipped to lead folks on a journey to hell, to the inferno, the worst bingo club in the world... I've got hell in me. Chaos is crawling out of every pore... and who is this sinister Malasso that we're dealing with anyway, shaping our journey? Are we going to hell or what? Are we all going to be slaughtered or what? I can smell something weird in all this. I can't hold all this together... my wife has just left me, my kids revile me, I'm the great joke of the industry, I'm up to my last hair in debt, my house is about to be repossessed, and here I am, bleating on and on to you... the best that can happen, I tell you Lao, is if I die on the journey... then I want you to take over, carry on without me, go on to the end, don't stop to give me a funeral, just make a good film for me, and stick my name on it along with yours. I want to die in Arcadia, in my own Arcadia, and that's making a good film. I want to die in my dream. The reality is too dreadful. So promise me, Lao, promise me that you will all get to Arcadia, that you will make a film worthy of the death of a poor wretch like me. Just promise me this, and I'll perk up, and I won't bother you any more, and not a word of despair will I breathe again, because I'll be content about my end. Will you promise me this, Lao?'

Twenty-one

Lao calmly heard him out, and without altering his expression one bit, an expression which had been neutral, with his eyes cool, his face fixed and still, his breathing unchanged, he said:

'Let me tell you the secret of the butterfly. The beauty of the butterfly's wings is a disguise, a secret language. To us they are just beautiful, but they conceal another purpose. They are used to communicate with other butterflies. The patterns on the wings communicate one thing to us, and another thing to other butterflies. But there is no deceit involved. We see the world in colour. Butterflies see the world in ultra-violet. The striations and patterns, seen through the eyes of a butterfly, consist of different intensities of blue. To the male butterfly, intense blues suggest an invitation for fertilisation. God knows what else they read as scripts or inscriptions on one another's wing patterns. They may communicate a whole range of things, personal disposition, nearness of danger, an entire alphabet of moods. We don't yet know how vast is this secret communication between butterflies, this secret speech. That is what art is. It's the hidden speaking to the hidden. All art is a secret language, a double language. And it does something other than what it appears to be doing. Sometimes it is effecting a secret cure on our spirit while being coruscating on the outside. Art has a sphinx-like quality, a faintly sinister quality. The sinister intelligence of the double function. Art is the ultimate spy. And you know that's what our journey is. It has many secret languages, and secret purposes.

And we'll discover them as we go along. And we'll fail often on the way. I don't mind failure; it's something to get past on the way to greatness.'

Twenty-two

When Lao finished with his little speech Jim stared at him with puzzlement on his face. They were both silent as the train wove its way past French towns, landscapes, houses, blue fields, over bridges, across yellow countryside. Husk brought the news that there had been a suicide attempt on the train. It caused considerable alarm among the passengers. A strange gloomy energy circulated the carriages as the word was passed on, bringing dismay and bewilderment in its wake. A suicide attempt? How? What could have caused it? Was it a man or a woman? The gender changed several times. Sometimes it was a man, sometimes a woman. Sometimes it was a member of the film crew. Other times it was a member of a business delegation.

Jim wanted to find the crew, to locate everyone and make sure they were all fine. The whole team was rounded up and accounted for, except Riley. She could not be found. Anxiety turned to alarm. The train staff were contacted; announcements were made over the train speakers. There was no response from Riley. The crew split up, and began a thorough search of the train. They searched the second class carriages, the toilets, the staff rest rooms, the baggage compartments, and they even extended their search to the train driver's cubicle. It seemed that Riley had disappeared.

The team sat down together disconsolately. Jim said:

'Who saw her last?'

'She was with me,' said Sam, 'loading the film camera as

usual. She went off with one of the cases, and that was the last time I saw her.'

'What was her mood like?'

'Mood? Mood? What do you mean mood? I wasn't aware of her mood. I was taking tricky shots of faces, shots of the countryside at an angle through the window. She's supposed to be my assistant, not to have moods.'

'I think she's been a bit depressed,' said Husk.

'A bit depressed?' cried Jute. 'She's been manically depressed!'

'Well, how did none of us notice?' asked Jim.

'Some of us did,' Jute replied.

'What's been wrong with her?'

'Everything...'

'So where can she have got to? There's nowhere we haven't looked. And she can't have jumped off the train because it's impossible to open any doors or windows. So she must still be on the train,' Jim said.

'We've looked everywhere...'

'She could be in someone's suitcase,' suggested Propr.

Everyone turned to look at him.

'Anything's possible,' he added, defending himself.

'Who attempted suicide?'

Now everyone turned to stare at Jute. Then it became clear that no one knew. They became silent as they contemplated the possibility that Riley had attempted to take her own life. They thought about her life in abstract terms, trying to puzzle out motives, reasons, secret distresses, troubles, and to reconcile this with her apparently sunny and chirpy nature.

'It wouldn't be like her though,' Jute said.

'I thought you said she was a manic depressive?'

'Jim, who isn't?'

'I'm not,' said Sam.

'I'm not either,' said Husk.

'I'm just manic,' said Jim.

'Maybe something to do with her father,' said Husk.

'What about her father?'

'They were close.'

'Is he dead?'

'No.'

'Dying?'

'No.'

'Then why did you bring up her father?'

'I just did,' said Husk defiantly, staring back at everyone.

'How pointless can you be?' said Propr.

'As pointless as I like.'

Silence followed.

'Maybe she's got a secret illness.'

'Like what?'

'Cancer.'

'At her age?'

'I know someone who's got cancer at twenty-three.'

'That wouldn't explain why she's completely disappeared though.'

'Maybe she's been kidnapped.'

'By who?'

'Malasso.'

'Who's Malasso?' asked Propr.

'Shut up!' said Jim.

'Why would he kidnap her? What for?'

'Maybe she's rich.'

'My assistant camera girl – rich? Unlikely!' said Sam.

'Maybe she's part of some terrorist group.'

'Why would she be a terrorist?'

'Why not?'

'Anybody can be anything these days, but the terrorist angle is too far-fetched,' insisted Jim.

'We're talking about her as if we don't know her,' said Propr.

'Do you know her?' asked Sam.

'No.'

'Do you?' Jim asked Sam.

'Vaguely, but come to think of it, no, not at all. She's very efficient, and works hard, that's all I know. And is good company.'

'Has she got suicide in her?'

'We all do, don't we?' said Husk.

'Speak for yourself,' came Propr.

'I don't think so,' answered Sam. 'There's something too happy about her.'

'It's the happy ones you have to watch,' said Jim.

'You're right,' said Jute. 'All the really happy people I know have attempted suicide.'

'Were they happy before or after?' asked Lao.

Silence followed the question.

'I'm not sure,' replied Jute eventually.

'Why is it relevant?' asked Jim.

'Because,' Mistletoe said, speaking for the first time, 'because Riley is standing right behind you, looking quite happy.'

Twenty-three

A hush fell on the team as everyone turned slowly around. They beheld Riley standing there, like a pixie, with an almost angelic expression on her boyish face. Her eyes were bright and wide open like a baby delighted by ordinary wonders. And her smile was fresh and frank, like the smile of children found playing in the woods. She had a look of such pure happiness on her face it gave the impression that she was a little deaf. Everyone stared at her in disbelief and astonishment, except Mistletoe and Lao. Something, a sort of light, radiated from her, transforming her. The radiance didn't last, but, for the moment that it was there, Riley appeared as her best possible representation. She had a sort of transfigured presence of her own joyful spirit, a transfigured afterglow. It was peculiar. And in that moment Jim drew a startled breath, and Husk recoiled in fascinated horror, and Jute gave a strangely exultant cry, as if a secret suspicion had been confirmed.

The silence deepened. The carriage darkened briefly as they passed through another tunnel. The train staff came rattling by with trolleys to collect the food and drinks, the cups and leftovers. Soon they were at the far end of the compartment. Riley didn't stop smiling the whole time.

Then Jim, in a very hurt voice, said to Lao:

'You mean you knew she was here all along and you didn't tell us?'

'Not all along.'

'But she was here for some time?'

'Yes.'

'And you saw her?'

'Absolutely.'

'Standing behind me?'

'Quite.'

'And you actually let us go on and didn't tell us?'

'Sure.'

'Why? Why?'

'It's quite straightforward really,' Lao said cheerfully. 'It's just that I think it's a good thing for people to live posthumously.'

'Posthumously?'

'Yes, and to hear what other people think of them while they're alive. It's good for all concerned. Frees people into the truth, and all that.'

'I think it's downright mean of you.'

'Only because you feel bad that you spoke your true feelings about her and she heard. You feel bad because you've been freed of your friendly hypocrisy.'

'You are the most pompous person I've ever met...'

'Besides, it was such a pleasure.'

'It was nastiness.'

'No, it taught me how much and how little other people's opinion of one matters. None of your opinions mattered about her a jot. You could have been talking about a complete stranger – me, for example. Anyway, she wasn't there that long, and barely heard anything. You can shuffle your guilt back into its cupboard. Besides, haven't we all got work to do?'

Jim turned to Riley. His face was faintly touched with sweat; it glistened. His eyebrows met, forming a sort of double bridge. His despair seemed to have partially diminished, or he was, for now, much less aware of it. And with some annoyance in his voice, he asked Riley:

'Where were you?'

'Me?'

'Yes, you, for God's sake.'

'Here and there,' said Riley with that charming smile of hers.

'Listen, we've been looking for you all over the damn place, in every single compartment. We thought something horrible had happened to you. Now you just show up here like that. We demand an explanation. Where were you?'

Twenty-four

Riley's smile grew more dazzling, more beautiful, and thus more mysterious. There was something uncanny about her. It was almost as if she were a shining angelic impersonation of herself. She didn't seem right somehow. It felt to the others as if a more beautiful persona had replaced her. She seemed possessed and taken over in some sublimely sinister way. It made most of them uneasy – uneasy with themselves, as if beholding one of the most peculiar mysteries of all, the miracle of self-transformation. For Riley seemed indeed transformed, as if the light of an odd revelation fairly hovered at the back of her head. And yet there she was, the same as ever. It was spooky.

Riley, looking briefly out of the window, her eyes returning, settling on Jute's for a silky moment, then on Sam's, then squarely on Jim's, then turning misty, nostalgic, forgetful, dreamy, said:

'I disappeared. Vaporised. Was abducted by aliens. Vanished into thin air. Disappeared into a pinpoint of light. Was possessed by an idea. Taken over. Locked in a brilliant space. Devoured by God. Released. Overcome.'

'You're talking gibberish,' said Sam.

'I'm sorry,' she said, still smiling, like a harlequin's assistant. 'Do you want the truth?'

'Yes,' came voices, almost in chorus.

Riley looked around, and for the first time seemed embarrassed.

'I don't know where I went. I blanked out and vanished and I feel wonderful. It's like I've been in a most wonderful dream.'

'What was the dream?'

Riley stared at Lao for a while.

'I can't say yet. It's so recent and so strange. It's probably of no importance. What I mean is that I can hardly remember. Was I gone for long?'

'Only for a couple of micro-seconds,' said Jim mockingly. 'You weren't missed at all. In fact, aren't you supposed to be doing something?'

Riley snapped out of her stupor, her beautiful stupor, suddenly. Her smile vanished, her light disappeared. Her dazzle dimmed. And her alert work persona took over. She became instantly efficient, alert, quick, and eager. Soon she was darting from camera case to camera, cleaning, preparing, loading, engrossed, like a printer's assistant. And about her every movement, her stoic and cheerful efficiency, and the absence of that angelic expression, about her now there hung the mystery of where she went, and where she had been.

Twenty-five

Filming was resumed. Lao made several addresses to the camera. The team preferred him in profile. They said that the lights did something odd to his complexion. He bore the gentle hectic ordeals of filming. He stared often out of the window. He contemplated Mistletoe's reflection, envying her freedom to conjure on paper dreams and dances, free forms and frozen forms, to create while travelling, to live in a delightful reverie, with that smile on her face, like the sphinx in sweet contemplation on a pleasant afternoon with no one around to trouble its lion-headed shadow on the Egyptian sands. And Lao, thinking of her sphinx-like nature, her being half in expression, and half in impression, smiled. Jim said:

'That's the most beautiful smile you've ever given to a camera, Lao.'

And Lao held the smile, thinking, as if stumbling on the truth for the first time, just how much we are our own photographic plate, thinking how the thought becomes the thing, thinking of the spiritual chemical power of thought that he had scoffed at so much, the notion, romantic and impossible, beautiful and magical, that you are what you think, that your thoughts take form in reality. And he wondered much about the successive overlay, combinations, qualifications, and the complex mathematics of all the thousands of different thoughts and their mixed materialisation either on the face, in the character, or in the lives of the thinkers of them. Does nature work out an arithmetic mean of all the thoughts, much like the bank calculates the mean of all your savings, debts, overdrafts, interests, and deposits the average in your account, or subtracts it? Is the visible life the deposit of all one's thoughts and deeds? Lao was smiling as he was thinking. He felt he had quietly entered a great open secret, a hidden law familiar to all, believed by some, practised by a few, a law as true and clear and as unalterable as the laws of motion, or the fact of gravity. Lao was smiling, and being filmed, as the train drew slowly into the city named after the feckless youth whose audacity in choosing between three goddesses unleashed the destruction of Troy...

Twenty-six

Pandemonium descended on the crew. Like an army fleeing its camp, or having to make a hurried crossing, the crew gathered its cameras, boxes, sound equipment, luggage, and sundry loads off the train, working in a frenzy, till station hands came and helped, for a fee. And feverishly, as if the city were a bus about to depart to the past for ever, the crew hurried to complete disembarkation. Everybody busied themselves. Lao, normally languid and distant, seeing his role as distinct from the filming crew, threw himself into fetching and carrying; and so did Mistletoe. All hands were on deck. Soon transition was effected from train to platform, from motion to stillness, from being hurtled through space to being substantial in time.

But there was no chance to catch a breath. Passengers streamed past everywhere. There had to be filming too of the arrival, the disembarkation, the passage through immigration into Paris. And the camera had to tell its lies, taking the same shots over and over again, till it looked like the truth. And Lao bore it all with the wily serenity of an Odysseus appreciating, on the journey, the truthful beauty of the camera's lies, and finding much in common with it within his own nature, so deeply committed to truth, so deeply understanding of the circuitous ways in which truth must be planted in the world in order for it to persuade, to fascinate, to capture the imagination, and to grow into an active force in the world.

Twenty-seven

And then, with all the bustle, the counting of luggage, and re-counting, with the crew members lost in work, they all forgot Jute's terror, and Riley's magic disappearance. Even Jim forgot his own near lachrymosal despair. Work had become god, directing their souls to outward goals. Everyone was lost to him or herself, except Lao, who had to make an awkward crossing, a crossing as difficult as fording a deep cold river. For now he had to ford human perception. He had to cross a terrain in the minds of people. He had to submit to one of his life's endless trials – the trial of colour.

He prepared himself for materialisation. For, on the whole, in the living moments, minutes, hours of self living in self, of his being dwelling in his being, of simply living in his life, Lao was almost never aware of himself but as a human being; and even then he seldom thought about being human, but merely was. His thoughts lingered and dwelled in realms humorous, realms philosophical, realms fictional, realms financial, when worried, as often he is, about finance. He dwelled in realms sensual and sexual, loving the body as much as the spirit, and loving the body of woman more than all other forms. He dwelled in realms of pure abstraction, thoughts without objects, dreams, notions, childhood moments lost in time's betrayals and exile. He dwelled in calm lakes with swans, in calm skies, with the birds of the clouds, among leaves and flowers of summer. He dwelled in the great suffering of millions in their broken places, in neglected continents. He dwelled in films loved, on faces that moved him, in books and paintings and music and art works that shaped him and shape him still, mostly in book-worlds, where things are real because abstract. Oh, he dwelled in the happiest realms of the spirit when not aware of it, and cultivated his cynicism as a perfect mask when not aware of his intrinsic happiness. But seldom did he dwell in the nature of colour, and colour differences on the great globe, because he lived, in spirit, within humanity's abstraction, within the oneness of it. He believed, deep down beyond thought, that all are one.

True, he had learned to live as a hermit, a recluse, and had as little contact as possible with the ugly things that induced suicide upon his soul. He had found this truce effective, this de-materialisation useful, this exile within England practical, this exile from colour grading a liberation, so that his mind could wander and be strong, and not burn with rage and self-doubt externally induced, but strong with the spirit soaring, free and powerful, like the mind of a child, or the casual notions of an Alexander on a quiet afternoon between momentous battles, serene master of the battles of daily life. He, Lao, dwelled thus, in a splendid unreality that made reality malleable, because he had come to secretly understand that all individual reality is unreality, and that we make our world with our thoughts. And with irony he thought of himself as a man and artist of the spirit and the world, a lover of the world, a giver and a learner, and a hundred noble and not-so-noble and sensual things beside, a dancer to life, a scholar of the serious and the light things, a poet, a thinker, a sexualist, a warrior, a fool, a free man, a broken-off island of God, a mind charged with the grandeur of all minds, a spirit courageous, a laughing being of joy, a divine victim, a clown concealer of discoveries and powers, but seldom, seldom, indeed, did he think himself a being, a man, a figure, reducible to colour, only to colour, definable only by colour, to a place on the spectrum, a light impression negative on eyes that in the hearts register such negation. He seldom allowed it, and when it happened, when he felt himself being painted into being, becoming only a colour, not a simple complex human being, like everyone else, when he felt this reduction, he experienced the strangest sensation of being snatched, for a mortal moment, away from Eden, into unreality, from childhood games and freedoms into adult imprisonments, from the hidden bliss of all creation into the eye's historical grading of pigmentation. Often it was not acute or violent or hostile, often it was merely being invented as an exotic, being projected upon, with the skin as a celluloid fantasy or nightmare, or a celluloid remembrance, or desire, or distrust, or illusion.

But now, with entry into Paris before him, facing the army of immigration control as he had done before in his life, sometimes with disastrous results, Lao felt himself materialise from the realm of pure being, of reverie, of selfhood, or the thoughts of happiness or despair, of money or love, of travel or wishing to be home, the vast run of human thoughts, that spin and merge, that dance and twine themselves through life's moments – he felt himself materialising from that realm of normal humanity into a state that Camus called 'humiliated consciousness': the consciousness of being automatically suspect, automatically distrusted, automatically de-humanised, less than humanised, demonised, because of colour differences, because of variety in nature's canvas, because of history, the eyes, what people read into the skin, illusions.

Lao approached his materialisation from pure selfhood to defensiveness with annoyance, with irritation. He called Jim aside and said:

'This journey is a quest, and in all great quests there are always trials.'

Jim was hassled. Sam wanted Lao in a shot with passengers streaming through immigration control. There were problems with the baggage handlers, and the heat, heavy-laden and multiplied by all the engines and the absorbent metal and the breathing concrete all around, exacerbated the general irritability. Jim said:

'What are you getting at?'

Lao said:

'There are invisible lines that society sets up which make some people more visible.'

Jim snapped:

'Stop being so damned philosophical. Get to the point.'

Lao said:

'I'm being philosophical to stop me being angry.'

'Angry about what?'

'There are many many invisible lines in the world. You cross the line without noticing it. You are unaffected by it. For you there is no line, no chemical reaction, no danger of being humiliated, insulted, bundled up and thrown out, shouted at, animalised, locked up in a back room with a gag that eventually chokes and kills. You wander through it all so unknowing. But if I go past the line a chain reaction is set off. The line is meant to weed out people like me, different people. The line trips me up. I get detained. I get questioned. It is a question of pigment. It makes pigs of people. My innocence is my crime. I am condemned at birth, because of a different sun.'

Twenty-eight

Jim was puzzled, the cameraman was impatient, Husk had to get many of the passengers to go back again so she could make sure they got a shot of Lao in a crowd. Lao said:

'Society always has invisible lines and nets, points of interrogation. Not so long ago being of a different blood, and belonging to the main trunk whence sprang the dreams of Jesus Christ, set off fatal chain reactions at those invisible lines. And the lines determined those who could live normally, as though life were a fairground for the favoured, and those who were bundled off to death camps, to be tortured, gassed, exterminated, made into soap, for the cleansing of society. I am one of those now who get in the way of such homogenising. You can't see it. You are not meant to see this process happen. But it is supposed to happen for your own good, and the good of your children. It is meant to be an invisible process. One is merely weeded out, quickly, efficiently, and carted off to some place away from the eyes of people like you. You aren't meant to notice, and all your life you haven't noticed, and for the rest of your life you will not notice, nor will your children, nor will any upright citizen. At the line, as I am being questioned, you will avert your eyes. You will think it's not your business to notice. And deep inside you will suspect that I have done something wrong anyway to deserve such treatment. You will have been thoroughly prepared for this by sundry information, released now and then, that is suggestive of my vague criminality and social aberrations. You will not care.

Besides, you will be too busy, you will be in something of a hurry. But, as you cross the line, you will go on, undisturbed, into normal life. And I will be dragged off to society's hidden inferno.'

Twenty-nine

Jim looked at Lao intensely, as if seeing him with new eyes.

'Are you trying to tell me that...?'

'Absolutely! Suddenly I spring to your eyes differently, don't I? Familiarity has somehow made you forget that different laws operate for the two of us. Here is a tiny moment of truth, old boy. In the eyes of friendship, we concede equality, even if some of your unexamined behaviour and thoughts don't quite live up to it. In the eyes of society, however, you are normal, and I am condemned. The moment I step into your world, which is not really your world but a bit of God's world, I suffer the impossibility of innocence. It's amazing; I sound like I'm in court, pleading my innocence with all the passion of the suspect. The more I state my case, the more guilty I sound.'

'So what do you want us to...?'

'Nothing. Do nothing. I just wanted to say this. To risk being awkward. To crack the complacency with which you regard this world. There are torments that we go through, because of a different sun, that you will never suspect. Society has an invisible hell which people like me are made to reside in, and it is normality. No one else ever knows this. And if I cry out about it no one believes me. That's because, blind and complacent as they are, they want to believe in the inherent fairness of their world, of the society and its laws. For me to cry out is to implicate them in this daily crime of silent genocide. They recoil. They accuse me of being paranoid. They assure me, quickly, that all their best friends were marked too by a different sun. They advise me to be better adjusted. I nod, and go on living in that different hell, under everyone's gaze, unnoticed even by my best friends, or my lover. It is perfect, this differentiation, this invisible hell. A perfection of condemnation, punishment, and absence of evidence. I am, by all accounts, living a fiction. If I cried out who would hear me down here, among the human orders?'

'What was that?'

'I'm rephrasing Rilke. Opening of the *Duino Elegies*.'

'Oh...'

Thirty

With a tender, smiling, ironic glitter in his eye and with the gentlest voice, Lao pressed on.

'And so, dear Jim, remember this when your next despair falls upon you. I live in despair all the time. Society has perfected the conditions for it. I live a life of endless stoicism. It's a wonder I get from day to day without suddenly going berserk and screaming genocide myself. It's a wonder I get from day to day without cutting my throat, unable to drag myself through one more minute of endless rage and humiliation and being excluded, judged, misperceived, colour-coded in all things, denied intelligence, suspected of crimes, burglaries, drug peddling, muggings, murders, robbing old ladies, of somehow always being in the wrong place at the wrong time, for the greatest crime of all which is simply being alive and breathing the air on this good planet. It's the little things that tip the balance. How often do women on seeing me clutch at their handbags, as if in my colour they read an inscription which says "Ecce mugger"?'

Lao smiled lightly, as if at a bad joke politely received. Jim shook his head and was about to say something, but Lao continued, gently, as if he were addressing a flower, and yet powerfully, as if addressing a fellow warrior.

'I live a permanent existential condition: most things conspire to deny me existence and historical validity. Sometimes I wonder if I exist, or whether I am not an invention, a nightmare invention, a regrettable invention, in the mind of society. Forgive this long speech, but so much silence about so much agony for all the days of my life was bound some day to unleash a torrent of words or deeds. And I'd rather get it all out now, once and for all, on this journey, so that I can return to my inner condition of Eden. I am word purging. I want you to hear this, and not forget. And then I want you to forget, and return me to my ordinary humanity, so that you don't commit the intolerable penance of bending over backwards trying to compensate for all the stuff one suffers in silence. Don't de-humanise me or insult my intelligence by trying to make up for the vile invisible laws that try to fuck up my pleasant existence. Just be more aware. Don't let them deceive you. Notice. Be alive. See through what they don't want you to notice. Don't sleep through life thinking that all is well under the sun and within society. If you see them dragging me off don't look away. If I cry out listen. Don't doubt first. If an unnatural mug-shot of me appears in the papers, and I'm accused of having murdered ten people, don't pass sentence on me in your mind because of the gruesome blown-up nature of the picture. Don't let them manipulate your response. Be aware that there are secret laws for different people, and these secret laws are carried out by the most innocent of citizens, by you, by your handsome sons and lovely daughters, and by most of the people I know and like. Be aware of how much you are secretly conscripted into complicity through fear, misinformation, lack of contact, casual demonisation, distortions of history, irresponsible novelists and journalists and poets and film-makers, and by certain pigmentational developments in photography. Being more human means being more awake to the beauties and injustices of life. I'm shamelessly on the side of beauty, of the spirit, of the heroic in humanity. But as a daily victim of the human capacity to cast one into darkness, I cannot deny humanity's capacity for meanness, complacency, and cowardice. I don't believe in being in a state of perpetual rage.

I choose humour, intelligence, imagination, elliptical angles, love, and wild wakefulness as my weapons. And I know that all these words are but as water poured into desert sands. You do not hear them. As the singer said – who feels it, knows it. Let's get back to work.'

Jim stood as if thunderstruck. He waved his hands about. His mouth opened, and shut, unable to speak for not knowing where to begin.

Lao said:

'One of my trials right now is simply whether as a black human being I'll be allowed in.'

Thirty-one

Jim stuttered, stammered, tore at his hair, crumpled in distress, stood back, waving his hands in the air, and no angels descended from the faintly renaissance clouds to help him, to bring illumination, understanding, instant empathy, so he could feel in his flesh and bones the full force of the troubling speech he had just heard. And so he fell back on his learned response, his declaration of colour-blindness and universal amity. He turned in a space that he wanted to vacate, the space created by colour, excluded from him, one he had heard so much about, that amounted almost to a negative myth and legend, the suffering and mistreatment of the other. And nothing in him, in his bounteous good nature, his universal love, his wonderful simple-heartedness, his profound sense of injustice, enriched by his life of sundry failures, made it any easier for him to empathise. He still felt excluded from the legend of the lifelong quiet humiliations inflicted on those burnished by a different sun. And this tormented him. He felt like crying out himself in his incomprehension. But Jim did the most extraordinary thing instead; he did something which sprang a gentle leak in Lao's eyes, a gesture he never referred to again, but which he never forgot, and which forever made him see Jim as a true brother on this earth, a brother in affection, in human fellowship, and across the artificial divide created by the eyes and thoughts of men and women. A brother on the great journey to Arcadia. Jim embraced Lao, and wept on his shoulder. And then he pulled back just as quickly, under the force of in-born embarrassment, and effaced speedily the evidence of tears on his face, and said to Lao:

'I'm being tried too in your trial. It's better to fail than to not see. Let's get back to work. Camera!'

And Lao, mingling with the crowd, with the gentlest smile of irony on his face, sauntered towards one of the more minor invisible lines in the world.

Thirty-two

Because of the presence of the camera, a peculiar thing happened. The law of different treatment became, temporarily, suspended. Lao's passport was checked only marginally longer than anybody else's – long enough to be noticed if you were aware of what was really going on, but perfectly natural if you weren't. Without the presence of the cameras, Lao would have been there for hours. Innumerable phone calls made, passport numbers checked, identity doubted, reality questioned. But the entry was painless enough, and the wings of good feeling brushed past his head as he burst into a little smile, saying:

'Ah, yes,' to an unfinished question.

And then, flowing now in freedom and lightness, regaining his state of grace, dancing on the sunlight of a romantic nation, followed by the tender gaze of the camera and the crowds, Lao wandered towards the train driver's compartment, to interview a man who loved speed but cultivated stillness.

BOOK FOUR

One

Stillness in motion, motion in stillness. Lao loved such paradoxes.

The train driver crouched in the doorway of his beloved train. He was genial and a bit hot. Crouching made him seem very tall. Sam loved the awkwardness of the angle, loved the idea of the train driver high up on the steps, crouching, and of Lao, low down on solid ground, talking up.

The conversation was difficult because the driver spoke in French, Lao in English. But the spirit was somehow right. Lao noticed the driver's eagerness, his willingness to comply, and his nervousness in front of the camera. It was endearing.

A paradox emerged and Jim, strangely animated by a new sense of mission, latched on to it, and wanted it amplified. Mistletoe stood away from it all, in an enchanted zone, drawing, sketching, seeing nothing but colours and emblems.

The driver's name was Luke. In his diffidence he revealed something interesting. It struck Lao that being a train driver was one of Luke's fantasies. But he learned that his greatest love was gardening. One was the perfect antidote to the other. The perfect complement. And so their conversation revolved round this circulum – the love of speed, the cultivation of a garden, of stillness.

Lao was struck by the facts: four times a week Luke spent most of his working hours with trees, roads, houses, and sometimes rain hurtling towards him at nearly two hundred miles an hour. While the train, from a distance, seemed to be an enchanted thing, weaving a graceful curve through languid countryside, in the driver's compartment, however, it seemed as if the whole world was throwing itself at him, tearing towards him, then vanishing past him, like a life lived at high speed.

Contemplated metaphorically, Lao couldn't help wondering if it didn't make of his life something of an hallucination: with the train as the mind dying in a dying body, reviewing in swiftness all the events of a life in time's duration. How swift is the passing of terrestrial things. How brief is a moment of time lived. How tenuous can memory be when things pass so swiftly. How illusory time must be when maintained at a principle of speed. How passing over the same landscape hundreds of times does not make it many landscapes, but the same terrestrial dream, incapable of expansion, or of minutiae. How a brief life, crowded with significant activity, becomes a long one. How speed makes of nature a painting, a stillness, thus contradicting the laws of visual motion. How a new life paradigm can be sketched from the rapid progression through a life that is swept along by the marriage of fate and will. How reality curves. How speed distorts time. How time distorts vision. How memory is a blur, but becomes a briefer blur when speed enters into the picture. How with such quickness it is impossible to linger, in memory, on a single witnessed incident – an adulterous kiss snatched in an orchard, a beautiful girl's skirt blown high by the wind and revealing curvaceousness in a flash too quick to translate into desire, a moment caught in a field of wheat, a man striking down another with a shining sickle, seen too fast to ascertain whether it was merely a farmer at work, a moment registered in wrong perspective, or a legitimately witnessed murder. Things that tantalise and infuriate the mind, and which also blot out of perception things subsequently seen. Because for something to be seen requires consciousness, and if the mind is dwelling on a previous detail it sees nothing afterwards but its own thoughts and reactions. And so much remains always unseen where there is much that fascinates the mind and eye.

To Lao it seemed a whole philosophy lay in the paradox, a life lived at speed, with many gaps in perceived reality, many things and events not looked at properly or deeply, which would later haunt one as fragments of dreams. A life viewed all mixed up, with dreams unclear. Life tending towards dream. Like the swift mysterious life of Alexander the Great. A life which because of so many mental puzzles, so many incidents to report, to perplex, leads the mind towards a preference for stillness. Preference for a life where things are given time to unfold, to reveal their hidden wonders or terrors. Preference for a life where seeing is just as difficult because it requires such stillness of heart, such patience, such concentration, such quietness of mind, such motionlessness of spirit.

Two

While he was interviewing the train driver, Lao was wondering whether a life really could conform to such a conscious neatness of shape. Or whether the internal principle of living needs that neatness of shape for itself and thereby creates an unconscious urge for its complement and cure that results in such harmony, such a circle.

Lao thought about the madness, the chaos, the sheer speed, the hectic movements, the unholy bustle and mixtures of modern life, the noise and pollutions, the rages and frustrations, the neuroses and the mad desires, the crazy dreams and the unquiet fantasies, the raving hungers and the babbling lovelessness, the mad motions of the spirit, the turbulences of the mind, the fevers of the heart and loins, the uprisings within, the tyrannies and the unjust democracies, the howling unfreedoms. Lao wondered if it weren't all these things that were giving rise to a new cry for peace, an unarticulated cry and scream for a homeland where the human spirit can be serene and where the best dreams can take some meaningful form. Lao wondered, as he listened, if the great boiling unconscious of humanity was not finding the notion that could heal its deep unrest in forgotten dreams of Arcadia.

He was thinking whether in times when life is so much like an hallucination, when cities are so crowded with monstrosities, wonders, and incidents, when things are too complex and complicated, when life is increasingly intolerable, twisting human beings into odd and fiendish shapes that they would not recognise in a clear mirror – he was thinking whether out of all the fury a new Arcadian ideal isn't the secret cry, the powerful cry.

Consider the speed and hallucination. The fragmented realities. The things partially glimpsed. The events witnessed but not understood. The welter of meanings and signs and auguries. Consider the loss of belief. The empty universe where the mind spins in uncertainty and repressed terror. The vacant sky where the heart sees nothing but desert. Consider lives crammed with confusion. With each person to his or her conflicting notions, philosophies, scraps and shards.

Out of all these juxtapositions doesn't the spirit throw out its own dream of clarity, its own clear countryside of the soul, its own clear lake mirroring the sky? Doesn't the spirit dream of its own slowed down pace, its own heaven, unrealisable in the world, but found within? For the world corrupts all ideals. And maybe only within can paradise be refreshed, can stillness be magnified, for the real forgotten self to come through, thus renewing life with renewed purpose and dream. Lao was thinking about these things while he was talking with the train driver.

And when Luke offered to show the crew his garden in the eastern suburbs of Paris, Lao was surprised and delighted.

Three

Jim was beaming throughout the interview. He had planted the idea of the offer, in Luke's mind, behind the scenes. But the journey had been planted on him, behind the scenes too. And he was beaming because he was following the instructions he had mysteriously found on his table on the train. Instructions outlining a trip through Paris. With clues concealed in the region of the train driver's house, if not in the garden. A conundrum and riddle that were part of the whole fabric of the journey, and Malasso's peculiar shaping of it.

And so while Lao was dwelling in the philosophies of the journey, his mind free from the anxieties of his life back home, Jim was thinking about fulfilling a double function. Getting footage for a film he was developing an increasing belief in. And following the instructions that had nothing to do with the film, but with something more unclear, but which he suspected involved money, or treasure, or robbery. Jim felt like he was in the movie of his life. Looking about him all the time, wondering if they were being followed, seeing suspicious types everywhere, Jim guided the crew through all the complications of transportation to the suburbs. For the first time ever he felt like he was at last living inside his life; living within it, not as spectator, or ironic commentator, but as the central actor, the lead, the heroic protagonist of what might be a comedy, a thriller, or a tragedy. Jim was a romantic: he hoped it would be an untragic tragedy. He wanted the impossible resolution, which life generally shuns.

Four

Paris had a subdued air that day. As they drove in the hired van through the great city they were all aware of the mood. It was a familiar mood. There had been bombings in Paris; policemen were everywhere. There was racist graffiti on the arch of the bridge near Luke's place, but it had been partially effaced. The crew filmed Lao and Luke as they walked through the grey area, with its grim concrete, its poor streets, its stale air, its defeated mood.

Lao was much surprised by the hidden aspects of the famous city as they drove to the train driver's home. He was surprised by the run-down housing estates where the poor lived away from the public glamour of the great buildings, famous boulevards, the imposing architecture of a great civilisation. He was struck by how what is taken as the heights of civilisation can conceal modern catacombs, ghettos, hovels, despair, inequalities. He was bemused by the persistence of such poverty and hopelessness so close to such ceremonial splendour. And he understood something of the rage that fed the fires of prejudice. And he sensed how much the rulers of the world, in failing to address the poverty of their own citizens, paved the way for future outrages to private images of their greatness.

As they went, Luke told Lao of his dream of moving farther away from the frustrations and bustle of Paris. He wanted to live in a stone house. Nonetheless, surrounded by run-down dreams, he remained optimistic about the future. Lao was struck by what a simple, hard-working, solid and dependable man the train driver was. He was also struck by how people were deeper than their jobs suggested. For, apart from being a train driver, Luke cultivated his garden, and on holidays he loved deep-sea diving. He often made dives to remote places under earth and sea, looking for relics of forgotten civilisations, Arcadias under the water, on sea-beds, among prehistoric fishes. He loved swimming and dwelling in such primordial dreams. He loved the quiet happiness of life beneath the deep waters. And as Lao listened to the simple train driver he sensed something in him of the reassurance of the quiet earth and the place of labour in humanity's balanced happiness.

Five

They got to the train driver's house and found it pleasantly chaotic. They were offered drinks, and the crew members made themselves comfortable with tea and cakes. They were introduced to Luke's wife, Odette, who was smallish, thoughtful, and solicitous. There was an air of tempered mourning about the house. There had been a recent death in the family and Odette's eyes were always on the brink of tears. Politeness helped with the transference of her grief. Her mother had died not long before and the house was still cluttered with her belongings.

Luke spoke of how much he hated their area. It was too noisy. He loathed the trains that rumbled past the back of the house. Lao thought it odd that a train driver hated the noise of trains.

Jim plied Luke with questions. It turned out that Luke travelled all over France and Belgium, and to London on the Eurostar. He never knew in advance where he was going to be sent, whether he would be driving a goods train at eighty miles per hour, or the TGV, or his favourite train, the Eurostar, at two hundred miles per hour. His spare time and holiday pursuits revolved round scuba diving with his family and the exploration of underground caves. He took his underwater exploration seriously. He had made dives into underground lakes and rivers, where he had discovered tusks of mammoths in places where human beings have never been before.

Odette had studied languages at a university in Paris, her preference being German and English. But she was too full of grief to talk for long. Jim asked Luke how he came to be a train driver.

'I dreamed of being a train driver from the age of seven,' he replied, in halting English. 'Near my grandmother's house I first saw the beautiful billows of smoke from the passing trains and I fell in love with the idea of being a train driver. I love driving through landscapes, particularly the landscape of Kent. I love passing through countryside. Trains are high speed nowadays. But it's not so fast when I'm driving through England because of its laws. It's nice that way because I see the English gardens and steal some ideas for my own.'

The conversation passed in a general way. Luke and Odette expressed their admiration for high technology and saw no contradiction between technology and nature, if wisely balanced. But it was the garden that most drew warmth from their eyes. It was the garden that most displaced the grief that lurked behind the rims of Odette's glasses.

Six

As the crew set up their equipment, and did their various tests, Lao was struck again by how unified people became when they went about a task. How the individual vanishes, and the work takes over. How like a flowing jigsaw a group becomes. How the turbulences and stresses within turned quiet under the hum and necessity of activity. How the self within, with all of its confusions, becomes the engine and charioteer of labour. How differences disappeared. How Jute forgot her fear of death; how Jim forgot his fear of failing; Mistletoe got lost in her sketches and dreams of future paintings. And Lao himself forgot his masks, his angles, and found himself genial and cooperative. He momentarily forgot, also, his affected cynicism, and he flowed with all the motions of the craft of film-making.

And in silent moments between takes, Lao allowed himself to survey the empire of his mind, to see which of the dominions within were in strife or threatening disorder. And he was surprised to find order and general calm throughout the vast dominions of his spirit. The internal governments were in reasonable harmony. A wise democracy reigned in all the realms. No tyrants had emerged, no dictators had begun usurping neighbouring states, and a universal concord prevailed. And he concluded that the gentle ideal behind his Arcadian quest was slowly filtering into and spreading through the vast empire of his spirit, and gradually returning the many nations to their true oneness, their natural unity.

Lao smiled at how temporary peace was in the realms without and the realms within, but he savoured the tender moments of sunlight in the train driver's garden.

Seven

Sitting at an iron table, Lao contemplated the little garden with a smile. He wasn't sure why it moved him so. There was nothing particularly spectacular about the garden, but a certain spirit prevailed. It was the spirit of care and humility, of shaping beauty within life's chaos.

Lao saw the terracotta pots of flowers on empty wine barrels. He saw the forsythias, the apple tree on the left next to the gate, the wisteria on the front fence, and the grape vines trailing from the railings. Lao marvelled at the variety of flowers and their cheerful intermingling. Luke had made a detailed study of English gardens and had created his own unique combination of flowers. His wife made it clear, with a gentle pride, that there had been nothing there before. That when they first came to the house the front was bare, plain stone and wood. Their love had transformed it so that it was now impossible to imagine that there had been nothing before. Such was the way of the creative hand, flowering life where bare stones lay, domesticating barrenness, beautifying concrete.

Lao gazed on the brilliantly blended colours of petunias and Ionian marigolds, of jasmine and chylous, of lavender and dahlias and geraniums. Lao, Luke and Odette were sitting round an iron table, under the meditative shade of a beech tree which Luke had planted eighteen years before. In the garden there were also apricot trees and silver birches and a cherry tree.

Lao smiled at the humorous notion of trees and gnomes

growing together. They had been made to look as if they emerged from the same roots, the same earth. There were gnomes all over the garden, giving the place a jovial feel. It was as if nature was smiling, enjoying a joke under the sun, always laughing, always aware of the essential humour of all living things. The gnomes seemed to be laughing at all stress, all fretting, all inflation of human things to levels of greater importance than they truly deserved. They seemed so like the domesticated representatives of Pan, of the satyrs, of the mischievous nature spirits. They reminded Luke and Odette that a secret smile hovers over all things mortal. And that beneath and above all tragedies there is a higher comedy that we can't be aware of because such divine smiling belongs to the greater perspective of nature and the nature gods, gods that transcend even history. For their sense of the essential comedy of all earthly things goes all the way beyond the stars and constellations to the immeasurable heavens.

Eight

Surrounded by the dahlias and Ionian marigolds, Lao told Luke and his wife a little about their Arcadian journey. Lao asked if they thought that humanity had lost its way and if it was possible to find some sense of paradise in a world so riven with wars, chaos, unbelief, and confusion. Luke's answer was simple: because of the impact of technology in all our lives, he felt that we needed to return to our origins, to nature. We needed space to work the earth, to rediscover our roots, to find some peace, and yield good fruits.

Jim liked the plain and simple answer. The crew helped with the clearing up. Gifts were exchanged. The couple's two children returned suddenly from a visit to friends. With a sense of sadness the crew gathered into the van, and drove off slowly, waving with so many hands from so many windows. Luke and his family waved back warmly as the crew journeyed onward.

As they left it occurred to Lao that the little family was a touching example of how very many people manage to create their own modest Arcadias. Theirs took the form of a simple garden amidst the noise, pollution, and stoniness of the modern age.

But Jim was all along also looking for secret clues. And in seeing too many, he found none.

Nine

It was when they went back to Paris, and settled into their hotel rooms, that the shadow of Malasso struck again. No one was sure how it happened. When the crew converged at the hotel desk for dinner in the evening, it was discovered that Husk had gone missing. The hotel staff hadn't seen her leave. Her key was not on the rack, but Sam said that he had seen her talking to a strange-looking man with hooded eyes and a black hat earlier in the evening. She had seemed distressed, he said, but he hadn't been alarmed because she had been that way for most of the journey, agitated about something, and extremely irritable. Husk's disappearance was very serious because she had all the schedules, the filming times, the appointments, and even the dinner arrangements for the evening at a nearby restaurant.

Husk's disappearance caused a tremendous sense of unease among the crew. The strange man she'd been seen with brought fears of abduction, kidnapping, and possibly worse. The name Malasso was whispered again amongst the crew. Propr took it very badly indeed. He began grumbling and pacing up and down the hotel lobby in his shorts that revealed his bandy legs. His wrinkled face with comic moustache became very peevish. He muttered bad-temperedly about the dreadful company he was keeping, the stupid idea behind the journey, the incompetence of the crew, about Jim's complete lack of leadership qualities, and the unprofessional nature of the whole expedition.

The crew members split up and went searching for Husk in

the environs of the hotel. When they couldn't find her they wanted to call the police. But Jim wanted to wait before taking such a drastic step. The last thing he needed was investigation and probing when so much was still uncertain, when any news in the press could wreck the entire project and end his film career which was already ending, it seemed, in disaster.

He tried to get everyone to calm down and suggested that they order drinks for themselves. No one calmed down. Sam kept fretting. Riley was jittery. Jute, convinced that tragedy was about to strike, began to see things, and spoke of catching glimpses of strange men spying on them, following them around. She claimed that they'd been followed all day, and that she had noticed a man with a black hat, hooded eyes, and a long scar on his left arm going into the train driver's house just after they left. No one paid her much attention.

Mistletoe sat at a table, sipping orange juice. She drew, in her large sketchpad, variations of a man in black with an exaggerated scar on his left arm. Lao remained oddly serene through all this, hardly saying a word, smiling in that faintly cynical manner of his. A profound unease dwelled among the crew. They avoided looking at each other. It could be said that because of so much that was unstated they had never disliked or distrusted one another as much as they did at that moment.

Ten

It was a sultry evening. The sickly fragrance of decaying roses wafted in from the derelict garden of the French hotel. It was a run-down place, the walls crumbling, the wall-paint murky and disgusting, the stench of stale heat and suspect latrines drifting down the stairwell. It was the sort of establishment that reminded one of the flea-pits that one reads about in nineteenth century French novels, establishments where hard-eyed prostitutes do brisk business. The odour of cheap sex, unwashed bodies, disintegrating condoms, and musty walls circulated freely. The rooms stank, and were small, and miserable, and conducive to the grim melancholy that prods the suicidal into terminal action. The rooms invited the occupants to evict themselves from life.

The languid warmth of the evening, the dispiriting odours, the unfriendly hotel staff, the abysmal conditions of their hotel rooms, the complete absence of the glamour associated with film-making all combined in the minds of the crew to produce a state of group stupor and despair. Slowly, paralysis crept over them. They sat there in the thickening gloom, tortured by hunger, crushed by an overwhelming sense of failure, and weighed down with shame.

Only Mistletoe was unaffected. The gloom provided her with dark shapes, the sense of failure with Hades-inspired images, and hunger fuelled the flight of her mind into a realm of enchantment. It was a realm she was able to enter at will because she had lived a life so rich with misery, mistakes and love that she had gradually found an art of creating pleasant places in her mind where colours are astonishing, where life sings, and where possibilities lurk behind all evil shapes. Unhappiness had taught her the art of happiness. And art had taught her the saving graces of escape into the enchanted countrysides of her mind.

Eleven

Lao steamed and boiled with rage. After a long time in the gloom, waiting for Husk to reappear, waiting for Jim to do something one way or another, he could stand it no longer. He said, very loudly:

'We all deserve to stew in hell, because we dare not create heaven.'

It wasn't what he wanted to say. This is what he wanted to say:

'You are all incompetent bastards. You deserve to stew in hell, because you are all such hopeless defeated indifferent cynical lazy-minded bums!'

He didn't say what he really wanted to say because, unknown to him, he was changing. The journey was changing him. The theme of the film was gently invading him. He was undergoing a slow contamination with a longing for a new way of being, a better way of living, a sense of peace and harmony. This, of course, in the future, would lead to civil war within. But for now he was being overtaken, gently, with a deep desire for a multiplication of his creative powers through serenity and quiet fearlessness.

He wasn't becoming moderate. He wasn't and would never lose his sharp edges. He was simply becoming a more effective human being. Nonetheless, his outburst disturbed the group. Propr responded first, standing up suddenly, his bandy legs framing the gloomy light that filtered in from the lobby. He began shouting.

'I've just about had enough of you and your smug pseudo-bohemian ways! Who do you bloody think you bloody are anyway!' he stuttered. 'What have you done to bring heaven or even decency to anyone, you lazy bastard pretending to be a bloody artist. I bring more decency to society tending my sheep than you do getting drunk and being sarcastic about everything...'

Then it was Sam's turn.

'I work harder than anybody in this damned room. I'm not going to be told to stew in hell by anyone, just because just because just...'

Jim broke in.

'Everyone shut up!'

'No, you bloody shut up!' bellowed Propr, eyes bulging.

'I'm quitting this hopeless film now, this very minute, I'm quitting...' cried Sam, sitting there, not moving.

'I'm quitting too. I quit before you quit. Bugger all of you. I'm leaving,' crowed Propr, not moving either.

'The film is dead, finished, end of story, end of Arcadia, end of everything, I never want to see any of you bastards again,' shouted Jim.

Then, suddenly, there was a strange silence, a profound silence. Nothing creaked in the entire hotel. The moment held its breath. Lao felt a shudder pass through him. Mistletoe stopped drawing in the dark, and listened. Jute drew in her breath. The fragrance of flowers thickened in the gloom, and in the dark a voice said:

'The lady you are looking for is outside. I think maybe she is crying.'

The group hurried out and found Husk in the middle of the street, fighting back her tears.

Twelve

They trudged off to dinner, with Husk in their middle, resolutely silent. Her thin lips had never been pressed tighter, her eyes had never seemed meaner, an evil mood emanated from her; and no one dared address a word to her or look into her Medusa face.

They sat around two joined tables outside an Italian restaurant. Jim had been there before and knew the food to be excellent. He was in good spirits. He was perfectly typical that way: once the main problem is solved, nothing under the sun interferes with the pure pleasure he takes in his dinner. He ordered wine. The group was grim round the table. Everyone was worrying about Husk. A family tragedy was suspected.

The evening was lovely as they sat out in the open, on the pavement, with a busker playing Mozartian notes on a flute nearby. Not far from them, at another restaurant, a magician was going through his turns. On the other side, on the left of the lively street, a harlequin was singing and clowning and performing somersaults. A troupe of gypsy musicians charmed the night with their pipes, ventilating an Andalusian air. The film crew ought to have been happy. To be alive, to be healthy, to be away from home, under a star-scented sky, in the middle of enchanted Paris, on a warm evening with a gentle breeze, on a filming trip, with the theme of charming a sense of paradise from the endless difficulties of an average life – these things ought to be able to tease out happiness from all but the most cussed of people. But the crew, locked in their habitual mode of being, seemed impregnable to such *joie de vivre*.

Lao was suddenly touched by this feeling from an angel's wing. He was touched with the romance of the city, and all its rich associations with literature, art, and freedom. He was touched with the spirit of eternal youth, and the love of beauty, and the ideal of excellence, and a feeling for the classical virtues. And, wishing to surround Husk's unstated sorrow with warm conversation, he proposed that everyone present reveal what their private Arcadia would be, whether a book, a person, a piece of music, a season of the year, a state of spirit, a country, a dream, an idea, or a vanished moment.

Thirteen

At first silence greeted Lao's proposal. No one moved. Mistletoe went on drawing. She was becoming her own ideal.

Then to everyone's astonishment, Husk suddenly spoke.

'If it's on my account you're all keeping quiet, then speak. Your silence only amplifies what I'm going through.'

Then all at once, and all in a rush, as if stones had obeyed an injunction to babble, as if brooks had all broken into so many soliloquies, as if vacant heads had become occupied by vying oracles, the group began to pour forth words, dissent, disagreement, collisions, agreements, in every direction, all unheard by the others, till Lao said:

'For God's sake, no one can hear anyone else. Can we be orderly about this?'

Then Propr took up the mantle, and spoke first. He said:

'Left to me, I don't understand this Arcadian business. I tend sheep. I am a plain man. I don't even think of myself as a shepherd. I don't understand things that I can't see. I don't understand things that I can't hear. I'm a practical man. Anything that doesn't turn into bread doesn't really interest me. I have children to feed. I'm getting on a bit in years and hate to admit it. The miracles of Jesus only make sense to me when he turns water into wine. I can always do with wine. The human race understands wine. Multiplying loaves and fishes is wonderful as well. A lot of starving people in the world could do with loaves and fishes. But the miracle of multiplying things is not a regular activity, and no one does it nowadays. So that bit is best left to intelligent human governments and enlightened politicians that care for the feeding of the world's starving masses. Personally, I'm only interested in money and contentment. I don't believe in going to far off places searching for ideals and ideal places and paradises that don't exist. I prefer to find what can be found here, where I find myself, in my backyard, in my home. I'm not keen on seekers. They are too restless and confused. Worse, they are lazy. They don't want to work. They don't respect the work ethic on which society is founded, and sustained. They want easy cures and easy miracles. They want complete instant solutions to all their problems. They don't want to work, or to think things through. And they tend towards fanaticism. They join cults, and abandon them. They are quitters. Always quitting their jobs, their relationships, their homes. Always quitting the latest idea they've just enthusiastically converted to. Always quitting their support for the latest band that offered them instant nirvana or an immediate oasis in music designed to make them part with their money and make the moronic musicians uselessly rich. These seekers are always joining, but never staying; always looking, but never seeing; always travelling, but never learning. They are always collecting interesting new bits of new-age information, but never integrating what they collect into a practical life. Seekers are actually very arrogant people, thinking that they know more than their fathers and mothers, always judging the previous generation, always thinking that they know better, that all previous knowledge is useless, that the system is useless because it doesn't give them the easy things they want. Seekers are usually very insecure and judgmental people who haven't grown up, haven't accepted the fact that they have to settle down and earn a crust like everyone else. They are always reading their tarot cards, burrowing into the I Ching; mispractising tantric sex, visiting fortune tellers, fiddling with astrological charts, delving cross-eyed into hermetic texts, wearing exotic clothes from Japan, Africa, India, Thailand, dabbling with Buddhism, Islam, Taoism, American Indian rituals, and the Kabbala, gulping down the latest sensational nonsense about Aztec temple prophecies, Mayan contact with aliens, hidden revelations of history coded in the Bible, messing about with tea-leaves, African sorcery and herbalism, the Kamasutra, and a thousand other such things that they never study deeply, always passing through, mixing the whole confusing mess, till they are a confusing mess themselves. They are always running from one guru to another, from one fraud to another. They listen, but never hear. They have plenty of information, but no understanding. They are thoroughly insubstantial and unreliable people. They have no philosophy, no backbone. They are easily duped, and they dupe others. They are selfish and egotistical. I know of some who spend their time chanting mantras for their own glorification and for selfish needs, chanting for success, without working for it, chanting for a lover without being able to inspire or sustain love. Seekers mostly have deep character problems: they have no character. They never stay in one place, always dropping out, always looking for fringe causes to justify their laziness, when all they really want is personal success by the back-door. These seekers speak of seeking for wisdom, but they have no humility. When they should listen, they talk. When they should be silent, they spout other people's ideas. They have no patience, or tolerance, really, and the wise words they quote are merely quotations, never lived through with consistency, and so they yield no tangible fruitful results in the real world. Nothing they touch endures. Nothing they plant grows. Because they never stick around to nurture anything. They are always flying off in meditation and talking about peace and freedom, when in fact they have no freedom, because they don't understand the place of money in the world. They think they are independent, but in fact they are the most dependent of all because they depend on all that they reject: society, tradition, civilisation. And seekers have no peace, because they are escapists, and sooner or later reality comes into the picture and exposes all their catch-phrases as hollow nonsense. No, my friends, I am a practical man. The world must be faced. Reality must be faced. Life must be addressed squarely. At some point a man or woman gets married and has children, and has to raise them. And even if they don't get married, or are single, and never have children, they still need to survive. They will grow old. They need money. They need solid values. Ideals alone can't do the job. And if they insist on feeding themselves on ideals alone, then they eventually get into a lot of trouble. And the worst is when seekers, facing the chilling years of failure, stop seeking. The worse is when they stop believing. They become the worst cynics in the world, and the bitterest people. God save us from them. I tell you this. Society has many faults, but the way it is is the way it is. And one must accommodate oneself to society, even if one is a genius. And so while you're all off searching for Arcadia or paradise, I'm coming with you purely as the sound man, sound in terms of film, and sound in terms of having my feet solidly planted on the ground. I therefore don't have a private Arcadia, only a life that I'm trying to live, and not all that successfully. But at least I'm not escaping my responsibilities by chasing dreams. Now I'd like some wine, Jim, if you don't mind. This Arcadia business has made me very thirsty.'

Fourteen

After his extraordinary speech, Propr turned towards the approaching waitress. A pungent silence hung over the table. The speech had produced a strong effect, a sobering effect. It seemed to have dampened the lively Parisian evening. The acrobats suddenly seemed listless. The applause they drew was desultory. A stale wind, bearing the odours of the warm gutters and faded perfume, wafted over from the Seine. The Mozartian busker's vitality appeared to peter out, giving the lovely flute melody a slowed-down depressing quality of jaded hopes and feeble yearnings. The gypsies were the only ones who retained their unique mercurial air, indomitable, with their bright colours still charming the evening with a magic undimmed by world-weariness.

Jim summoned the waiter and ordered four bottles of white wine and rosé. Nervously the gathered crew consulted the menu. Those who could read French did so loudly, sharing their understanding of the menu with those who didn't, much to the irritation of the latter. Lao couldn't read French, and peered at the menu with a studious air, his mind vacant, a condition which produced interesting results, for he found to his quiet pleasure that he could make out what was beef and what was chicken, what was potato and what lamb, without trying. He concluded that being in a fine mood sometimes compensated for ignorance.

Mistletoe, being able to read French, confirmed his intuitions. Jute glared at the menu reproachfully, clearly resenting the obscurity of the French language and its unwillingness to yield to the common sense of English. One could see her eyes trying to find the English words hidden within the French words, without much success, and she was obliged, as a proud Northerner, to order blind, as it were, on pure speculation.

Soon the waiter came round, and orders were laboriously taken. Drinks were poured, a toast was proposed to the success of the film expedition, to the Arcadian notion, and to a happy outcome. Then the wine was drunk. Another silence ensued. Then, clearing his throat, Sam, the cameraman, spoke next:

'There must be a personal reason why Propr talked so passionately about the suspect nature of seekers. And he speaks well and largely truthfully about many of them. Maybe deep down Propr is a secret seeker, or an ex-seeker.'

There was some laughter round the table at this. Propr's only response was an enigmatic twitching of his moustache. Sam continued.

'I know a lot of seekers. They are always back-packing their way round the world. They are always hurrying to see things. They go to exotic places, take part in some ritual or other, meet others, hook up, carry on their journey to the next place, and they only have what they saw and what little they did as their experience. They are always travelling through. They never travel into. They insult the cultures and philosophies and religions of others without knowing it. And they do so in complete earnestness, naïveté, and innocence. But they are one kind of seeker. There are other kinds, just as intolerable. They are seekers that stay at home, seeking for things in books, in history, in the past, and they too are just as lost, just as confused as the seekers that Propr describes. These other seekers don't look at the world. They don't look at nature. They don't look at their fellow human beings. They think that books are more important than people.

They think that books are more important than life. They take little interest in politics, in fashion, in the young, in outsiders. They are blinkered and blinded by too much knowledge that isn't really wisdom. And what they know, what they call knowledge is not much use to them and not very practical. I don't claim to be as practical as Propr. I don't have a farm, I don't tend sheep, and I'm not a shepherd. I believe in the senses, in sensual things. I suppose I'm a sort of romantic. I like impossible things. Things that are easy to do bore me. Things that are easy to get bore me. Maybe that's why my life is not so great. But that's the only way I can be happy: seeking for impossible things, and never finding them. I am restless. Something deep is missing in my life. I don't know what it is. I used to think it was beautiful women, but when I get them, and have them, the thing I'm looking for, that's missing in my life, seems even more acute. As I get older a terrible longing for something that I can't give a name to takes greater possession of me. Sometimes I wake up in the middle of the night in great panic because of it. I can't stay still because of it, and may well die looking for it. That's my nature. I don't know what it is. It isn't money, career, family, success, or achievement. Everything seems hollow in relation to it, this thing that's missing in my life. Sometimes I have a dream and I'm in a room as immense as the universe and I can't move because of the terrible weight of my body and yet there's something in me that wants to be free in that immense space but that's trapped in my body and it's absolute agony, that unfreedom, that imprisonment in the body. I wake up in a great sweat, and in a sort of immortal terror. One can't escape the truth one must face in one's dreams. At the end of the day there's nowhere to hide. One either lives or dies. If one dies, one dies in such ignorance, without having tried to penetrate the wonderful mysteries of life. Wasted time in the university of experience. But if one lives, then sooner or later one has to deal with the ache and the problem of that thing missing deep in one's life, that deep longing. And so I'm sort of sympathetic to this Arcadia thing. I've never heard of it before, and that's enough to make it interesting and fascinating to me. It seems to me that most people, if they look deep enough within themselves, have an elusive something that they are looking for, an elusive peace, an elusive happiness, a crucial bit of the jigsaw of life. A need for meaning. A greater sense of purpose. I don't know how one can be human without this longing, this yearning. To be without it smacks to me of a singular lack of imagination, of sensitivity, of humanity. I too like bread and wine and things you can touch and feel and see and measure. I'm not averse to money, and like everyone else, I too dream of fame. But fame is not it. I should know. I make films with the famous, and there's not much to them apart from being famous. It's we who confer this condition on them. It is not something they have. Fame is a sort of perfume that some people have sprayed on them. The fragrance is nice and mysterious enough while it lasts, but it soon wears off and they have to live with their own natural ordinary smells. And one can only hope for their sake that their natural smell is good. But it usually isn't so they keep needing more fame to cover up the bad smell of what they really are. I think it is better to smell good naturally. Call it natural fame if you like, natural charisma, natural shine. There are people who have that natural fame, that shine, and when you encounter them it's like meeting one of life's true stars. These are developed souls, I think, quietly astonishing people. And it's got nothing to do with looks. The camera loves that natural shine, and I trust the camera. There are things that the camera picks up that aren't visible to the ordinary eye; it picks up people's auras, their true nature, their true light. It's hard to explain, and it doesn't take the form most people think. Only a few can pick up on this mysterious radiance. And so while I'm on this journey I'm prepared to be open to the notions that inspire us because I sense that life is empty without some sort of dream, some enchanted purpose, without some sort of intangible something. And in my time as a cameraman I've experienced some pretty strange things to do with light that tells me that there's more to life than we think there is. The fact is that, in spite of my ponytail and my air of being a sensualist, I'm just as lost and confused as anybody else.'

Fifteen

Sam had finished, and emptied his glass of wine, and lit a cigarette, and smoked with an air of romantic intensity. He fitted his surroundings well. There was something about that Parisian evening, with its muted lights, its air of festivity, its sensual hum, which Sam found conducive to wine, smoking, and an honest declaration of his improvisatory view of life. He was aware that he had begun his speech in reaction to Propr's speech, but he had not reached a conclusion that came from deep within him. He still felt that what he wanted to express was deep inside him; and this made him a little frustrated.

Lao, with a playful touch of malice, had developed this idea of Sam as fabulously talkative. It was based on their first meeting, on a shoot in Cornwall, when Sam had buttonholed Lao for two hours, outlining his theory of the place of suffering in art, the idea that suffering conferred authenticity. It was Sam's big philosophy then. Time passed, and life happened to Sam, and he became less talkative. Now he doesn't talk so much, but the air of talkativeness still surrounds him. Maybe he talks much in his mind. And now Lao shapes their conversations so as to encourage the shortest possible replies. Even Lao noticed how much Sam had changed.

Sam wasn't much given to talking any more, and had spent most of his professional life displacing speech into what can be caught in camera angles and oblique shots. He had deliberately made himself less literate in order that the camera should do all his philosophising for him, all his poetry for him. He was a victim of his own dedication to an aesthetic, to a doctrine of professional life. And so he drank some more, and got a little drunk. And while others made their contributions, saying things here and there that he would have liked to have said, he got resentful, grumpy, and insular. And it was only the wine and the mood of the city that prevented him from being wholly locked in himself. And so he listened with interest while the food was served and other crew members spoke of their private Arcadias.

It came as a surprise to all of them, however, considering how sarcastic, how distant, how distrustful she seemed, when Jute spoke next. She waited for a suitable pause, for the long silence after Sam had spoken. It would be just her way – to wait for a long silence, and to speak as if throwing a gentle grenade into a tea party. For she concealed within her apparent slowness of manner a sly sense of the subversive, of the angular, of always coming in from the blind side, out of the wing, beyond the periphery of the eyeballs, inflicting damage before her presence was registered, and retreating just as fast into the shadows, as dangerous and as insouciant as ever. And so, with cadenced and cool intensity, she spoke, saying:

'I like work. I think work is everything. I think work is Arcadia. Too many people hate work, they want it all easy, they want it all for free. I think that to have work to do, work that you like doing, is a good thing. I grew up knowing how empty is a life without work. When my father was laid off that's when he became inhuman. That's when he became a monster. We've always worked. Humanity is a working principle, a work-in-progress. Work is where I sing. I like being involved with things, with people. It's not fashionable to say this, I know, but even love is work. And if you don't put work into love then it fails, it falls apart. People want things all soft and easy. They want love to

174

work out without working at it. They want life to work out without working for it. I don't know if I'm a seeker or not, a dreamer or not, but I don't understand anything that's mystical. I understand things that mean something to people, things that can help them, things that bring them together, things that make them work with one another. I don't understand miracles. I don't understand magic. I don't understand dreams. And maybe I'm a contradiction. But I understand Sam's yearning. It's something I get only when I'm working. I stop and think 'Am I missing out on life, am I missing the real picture, is there another kind of life I can be living, is there another better way of being me, Jute, is there more to life than running up and down these corridors and arguing about budgets?' But then I go back to work, and carry on, and find some kind of satisfaction in it. But if I'm honest I'd say that there are more and more moments in which I begin to feel that there is something beyond work. Don't get me wrong. I'm not a workaholic or anything. I like a drink as much as the next person. I love my holidays and I think travelling and visiting other countries and seeing other people's traditions and way of life is a wonderful thing. I really love it. Me and my mates, we get a lot of travelling done. But at the end of the day it comes back to work, because if it wasn't there I wouldn't know what to do with myself. I wouldn't know what to do with time. I hate being idle, not doing anything, being bone lazy, leeching off other people. I also think we should be careful about seeking. Sometimes the best thing is right there in front of you, right there in your life, and you're not seeing it. Then you lose it. Sometimes the best thing is right there in your land, in your patch, and too much seeking can take you all round the world and make you miss out on life. I think life is quite simple, really. And I like life simple. Too much fretting and worrying oneself about things is a waste of time. Simple pleasures, that's what matters. And appreciating what you've got, the friends you have, the love you have, the health you have, and the job too. And so, for me, if I have an Arcadia, it would have to be something simple, something that's there, that's here, and something that I can never lose. But I can't say what that thing would be right now, and I won't be pretentious about it.'

Sixteen

And just as suddenly as she began, she ended. And ended on a note, typical of Jute, calculated to set proceedings on an awkward edge. No one speaking after her would want to fall into the accusation of pretentiousness, and so everyone would be aware of the underlined censoriousness of her contribution. That was Jute's way. To function as censor of excess sensibility, to be a corrective, to keep things balanced, to make sure everyone balanced the book of their actions, speech, gestures. And then to give a good account, without mystification. More than a bureaucrat, she was the steadier of people.

A long difficult silence followed her speech. Cutlery tinkled, wine gurgled in glasses, water was drunk, food was devoured. The evening darkened, the lights brightened. Happy voices rose drunkenly and fell all around. Paris was in bloom. Paris was showing off its charms. Paris was weaving on the gentle breeze, softening thoughts, fluorescing desires, waking the slumbering youthfulness of its visitors, freeing restraints, liberating knotted libidos, bringing to life what was crabby, seducing an imagined elegant way of being out of the stiffening attitudes of revellers. And Paris listened and waited at the table, with an amused and faintly condescending expression on its face, as the silence drew out between the crew members at dinner.

Time wove its spell around the impatient Paris. Those who hadn't spoken yet felt the pressure to speak, or they might afterwards find themselves making the speeches they hadn't made way into the night, into their sleep, and throughout the next day, making the unspoken speeches endlessly.

To everyone's surprise Jim spoke next. He spoke as he had never spoken before. He spoke as one under the spell of an idea expanding in his being and changing his inner terrain. Maybe it was the wine. Maybe it was the attentions of the bemused city, sitting in their midst, beautiful and easily bored, eyeing the festivities of the heart where a Helen is always stirring. Whatever it was, Jim spoke as if quietly touched by something mysterious, enigmatic. His voice lowered, till it was almost a whisper, and everyone strained to listen. And the invisible Paris signalled that the universal hum of the festivities be lowered a little so he could hear.

Seventeen

In an enigmatic whisper, rising now musically, now lyrically, Jim
began, saying:

'There are many kinds of gurus. In India a guru is that which
awakens. And so it can be a person, a book, an object. A child can
be a guru. Anything can be a guru which awakens you, which
opens up enlightenment in you. I begin with this because to me
the most important thing is not that which does the awakening,
but the awakening itself. But we must praise and acknowledge
that which helped the awakening. And so I want to praise and
thank all of you tonight, for in everything you have said so far
you have all been gurus, awakeners. This journey too is a guru,
and the Arcadian notion, so very different from the previous
ideals that have clustered round the idea of Arcadia, is a wonderful
guru. For, as Lao will tell you, and it was his idea to begin with,
though he is being very modest about it in his typical masking
kind of way, as Lao will tell you, Arcadia has always been associated with the pastoral. Whereas our notion of Arcadia, which
unfolds and becomes more mysterious every day, is something to
do with a quality of enchantment, a sense of a lost inner paradise,
a way of being which belongs more to the future than to the past.
The true Arcadian notion belongs to the future of humankind;
we haven't realised it yet. We haven't discovered it yet. And
Virgil's idea of it, as Lao points out frequently in our private
discussions, is very much an early intuition of the full human
possibilities of the Arcadian dream. I have often wondered

whether this notion of a lost inner or outer paradise is something to do with the past or a premonition or a dream of something yet to come, a thing of the future, as yet unmade. So we on this journey are trying to redefine Arcadia, using the past notions of it as a guide, a beacon. We are transforming the dream. I say this now to offer a few pointers to all the crew, to Sam in his search for the most beautiful and clear images, to Propr who, in spite of his disbelief, must find the right sounds, and to Lao himself who silently threatens us all with absolutely no contribution to this discussion – that Arcadia may be in the future, it may be ahead of us. Our lost childhood, our lost golden age may be ahead of us too, to be rediscovered by all mankind, in a higher condition. And so it is both a deeply private thing, a private quest for meaning and happiness, and a deeply public thing, a universal need for harmony, balance, and enlightenment. Speaking personally, for I should declare my hand, I am like Lao here, and in complete agreement with him. We all need something. We may have been born complete but we lost something along the way. That thing can be found again, better. I am a professional man. My professional life hasn't been the most successful in the world. My hair is falling out. But as I feel myself nearing the grave, I feel it more than ever necessary to make my peace with failure, with this earth, with life, with death, with fear, with limitations, with illusions, and with the universe. Our Arcadian ideal has something in it by which I can make this peace. In other words, I want to learn how to die better, in the hope that, for the days left to me on this earth, I may learn how to live better. Now can someone pass me the asparagus, please, I haven't had my share yet.'

Eighteen

Gentle laughter sounded all around as Jim concluded his speech. And when the laughter subsided, thoughtfulness and silence prevailed. Jim's words had moved everyone, had touched them in surprising ways. Husk suddenly began to weep. She wept with her face upturned, and a smile on her face. She wept silently, the way lovers do when they feel too deeply the love that overwhelms them and when they can find no words to express it. Propr was more thoughtful than he had been in a long time; and his moustache rendered his thoughtfulness comic. Sam stared straight ahead, in an ascending straight line that led to the constellation of Orion. Riley, unused to such philosophising over dinner, having spent her most profound moments, it seemed, in nightclubs and on beaches, in fleeting gropes with perfect strangers in far distant lands, sat in a state of curious possession, as though listening to strains of music she had never heard before, or had heard before but which made no sense to her, but which were beginning to reveal some peculiar inner beauty that puzzled her.

Mistletoe had a smile on her lips, a radiant and enchanted smile that so delighted the invisible Paris. It was her smile of eternal happiness, of gratitude for having lived so close to the edge of personal disasters and miserable decisions and come through them and found art as companion and solace, and a great friend in Lao. For these reasons happiness came easily to her, and when it did she was like a little star, a tender sun, beaming with undisguised beneficence. It was a smile that irritated Lao often, for reasons he could never fathom. But when he caught a glimpse of it out of the corner of his eyes it enchanted him too and revealed to him more than he could bear of the beauty of her spirit, and the kindness of her soul. But Lao was not aware of it then. He had listened to Jim's speech with a slight frown on his forehead, with a mildly sarcastic masking of his sympathy, and with grimly impassive eyes. He had eaten little, drunk much, and was determined not to speak. Jute, whose face was also of granite severity, when even at her most sympathetic, said:

'Jim, what you said was very moving. I wish I could feel it too. Maybe I will, as the journey progresses.'

Nineteen

More silence followed. The breeze had mellowed. The mood of a Chagall painting faintly flavoured the air. Circus folk had joined the acrobats on the festive street. Passers-by had given money to the busker, and he renewed his Mozartian fluting, weaving the most teasing enchantments through the air. Prancing young men and beautiful young women charmed the eyes. Old men and women, re-inventing their youthful selves, with slightly perplexed looks on their faces, moved through the flowing throng. And Husk, who had stopped weeping, and had just gulped half a glass of red wine, said:

'If I have an Arcadia I would say it is love.'

She paused. Her hard and tough and tight-lipped face suddenly crumpled and became distorted as she attempted to continue.

'I just want... I just want... forgive me, I'm not usually... usually... like this... I never show anything... never... But I just want my love... my love... I want my love back...'

And she got up, and fled from the table, in strange grief and broken-hearted anguish. She ran into the gaiety and cheerfulness of the Parisian evening. It was a gaiety that is indifferent to the misery of the heart-broken, because the invisible Paris, though young and beautiful, though eternally enchanting, prefers those who are happy in love, much prefers the company of the cheerful. His eyes are too fixed on the scenes of human celebrations and fiestas to notice the battles and woundings of the heart. And some think the invisible Paris heartless for that reason, but it's just that he is the eternal personification of the spirit of youth, who prefers beauty to all else, and happiness to misery. He follows what charms his eyes.

Husk was unnoticed by Paris as she stumbled through the crowds. Most of the crew members, led by Jim, ran to find Husk to console her.

She was eventually spotted wandering down a side street, alone, surrounded by tender blue shadows. But she was not weeping any more. And when they came upon her she smiled. Her hard eyes were harder in her smiling. She said:

'I didn't mean to spoil that wonderful discussion. Forget that this happened. I was just following a lovely white cat. Someone had painted her tail blue. Oh, you *all* came after me. How *kind* you all are. Let's go back to our discussion. I'll behave from now on.'

Twenty

And silently they led her back to the restaurant.

The invisible Paris had left their table because the magic circle had been broken.

With the serious and comic visage of a drunken Cerberus, a scaled-down Cerberus with a misbegotten moustache, Propr sat guarding the food and wine. Propr was fairly drunk now, and half stood when they returned. And when all were seated again it soon became clear that the Arcadian charm they had unknowingly woven about them, because of talking about it, had vanished, blown away by the gentle breezes.

The charm hovered over another circle three streets away where friends were half way through a delightful dinner, outside a celebrated restaurant. Poets, novelists, film-makers, and critics, they briefly touched on the merits and demerits of a recent translation of Virgil's *Eclogues*. They tore it apart, then passed on to the subject of a sensational new film, without being touched by the Arcadian magic drifting about them in the breeze.

The invisible Paris, who hates disasters, scenes, misery, cheerlessness, funerals, break-ups, divorces, arguments, bad taste and bawdy jokes, had also flown away from the film crew's table. Upon their return none of them attempted to take up the broken discussion. They all sat around gloomily staring at the plates of partially devoured food, with an absence of enchantment in the air.

The magic had gone. Nothing more now could be drawn out

of the Arcadian dream. The ideal would not reveal itself where there is no magic, where there is no sense of communion and good cheer.

And so the breeze changed. The flautist quietly crept away. The acrobats somersaulted into the dark. Harlequin vanished into his element. Some gypsy girls lingered, and pursued, here and there, in plaintive tones, the coins of sympathy. Jim called for the bill. Lao stared at a silvery light that was hovering in the breeze. He was not aware of what he was looking at. Mistletoe was relieved that she didn't have to speak or to elucidate her private Arcadia. Riley was pleased too, because in spite of having heard the word so many times, she didn't have the faintest idea what it referred to, or what it meant. All she could think about was swimming in the blue seas of summer.

The bill was paid, and in silence the crew made their way back to the hotel. They went to their various lonelinesses and dreams. They went to their shabby little rooms that were still redolent of the cheap sprays that disguised previous encounters.

Twenty-one

They went from little Arcadias to large ones; from a train driver's humble garden to the vast cultivated acres of a king.

But before that they had a day off. They were entering the spirit of the journey. Away from their homes, from their moorings, from the familiar, they were becoming more alive, more vulnerable, and in some ways more open.

They had slept and dreamed, each in their different ways. And each had woken to a day peculiar to them. Lao and Mistletoe had woken early and wandered the streets of Paris at dawn. The smell of the city at that hour was so new to them. They watched the road sweeps at work. They watched the waiters bringing chairs out to pavements and smelled the fresh coffee rising from the cafés. They watched the early risers and the dawn workers, people of all races, as they hurried on to their workplaces. They seemed so different from the early risers back home, and even the sight of them here held a certain charm.

The city was waking slowly. The armed gendarmes outside the Élysée palace paced up and down, fully armed, and stared at them with mild suspicion as they went past twice, looking for a good café where they could have a nice breakfast. They found one, and Mistletoe chatted to the tall waiter, asking about news of the city. They were the first customers of the day. All about them chairs were still upside down on the tables.

Lao sat passively, staring into the pages of Virgil's *Eclogues*. He was staring beyond the words, beyond the abstract marks on the old cream pages, into something beyond the words, the reality that lurked behind them, but not in them. He was thinking what a magic operation writing is, what a symbolic, a signic activity it is, how it is so secretly based on the interpretation of signs, the translation of signs into a mental reality, an inner reality, an inner world. He was thinking how much the words create the worlds within, and the worlds within enrich the world without. Reading too is a magic operation, a translation, an act of mental creation, or miscreation. An interpretation. A connection. All reading, he felt as he stared into the labyrinth of the pages, is the challenge of magnifying what is silent in the text. It is reading with an inner magnifying glass. Reading what is there and not there. Reading the margins, the gaps, the spaces between the lines and between the words. Reading the punctuation, the ellipses. The invisible words too. Or else, reading is passive. And so reading is a hymn to the challenge of the imagination and the intelligence, humanity, and sensitivity of the one who reads. They make the world within the words greater or smaller. But the artist shapes and compresses and hides the signs that spring from their coiled places, and makes them capable of such magnification when the reading mind is open to them and meets them with commensurate creativity. Reading well is as creative and as rare and as rewarding as writing well. And Lao felt that the world was much like that too. Life, the world, society, reality, history is a sprung text that we endlessly learn how to read better. Experience is a living text written in our immortal memories that we endlessly learn how to read better. Some signs are harder to read, and we need to learn more to be able to understand them. Some texts dwell in disguise, and we misread them, or don't see them at all. And others live in quiet hiding, among the simplest things, and yet they are connected to the most profound things of all. How alive and how free and how enlightened one must be to be able to read the texts of living and the text of books, Lao was thinking, ruefully, as he stared into the pages.

Mistletoe drank her coffee, thinking much the same things, but in relation to art, to painting. She was thinking how reality is one vast complex painting, a living painting, full of riddles and meaning, of enigmas and hinted fates. She was thinking that there was as much chiaroscuro in life as in painting, and as much depth, concealed interiors, as much sfumato, as much smokiness around key significations that don't necessarily announce themselves as such. There was as much mystery hidden right on the surface of things, difficult to see like all deep things that dwell transparently on the outside, extending their realms of meaning and ambiguity in the deepest places of the person who looks. And there was as much simplicity in the depth of things, the utter simplicity of an absolute truth, dwelling in the greatest depths. So that to one who knows how to make and how to see, the truth of things is both right there in front of you on the surface, transparent and clear, as well as deep down where only the bravest and the wisest can go. All true seeing is a testament to the person who sees. You see what you are. You create what you are. You read into a painting, into the world, what you are.

These two creatures ate their breakfasts, and drank their tea and coffee, in absolute silence, staring at the world, at passers-by, at the café owner, at the prints on the walls, at the chairs and tables, at the people hurrying past outside the large glass windows of the café as if they were in a different reality, a separate space.

These two creatures stared at the things going on outside as if they were flowing inscriptions, living hieroglyphics, motions in a vast living painting, pregnant with mystery.

They stared at everything like children. In that Parisian dawn all the world seemed an infinite text which the spirit reads, but the brain doesn't.

One can be ignorant while still inwardly growing.

They stared silently as they woke with the waking of the city.

Twenty-two

The other crew members had their various tasks. Jim went buying gifts for all the people they were going to interview on the journey. It was something he loved doing, finding imaginative and relatively cheap gifts for people. It was based on his understanding that if he didn't have much money to pay people, instead of insulting them with paltry sums, he would honour them not only with gifts but also with the care and love that had gone into choosing each one, so that the gift matched the recipient.

Jim went up and down Paris, to the different markets. He went with Husk, who gave him advice on gifts for the women. When Husk wasn't shopping with Jim, she was working with Sam. She sorted out the schedule, phoning up people, making contacts for future encounters on the journey, helping with the accounts, arranging all the logistics of the long trip ahead. Husk threw herself into her work with an intense and bitter severity to escape the fiery pangs of her broken heart. She spoke to no one about the nature of her anguish, nor did she give hints or details of what ailed her. Often she had to stop what she was doing and hold onto something solid. As if to prevent herself falling because of the sheer weight of emptiness in the pit of her stomach. She worked like a stoic, but without the stoic's philosophical serenity.

For the rest, their tasks were specific. Sam had his cameras to look after. Riley followed whatever instructions Sam gave her. And Propr, not having much to do except keep his sound equipment clean, decided to make a day of it. Along with Sam and Riley, he disappeared into the lures of Paris. They were not seen again till the evening. And when they materialised they were somewhat red-faced and drunken and merry. The crew ate separately that night, and in the morning the Arcadian journey was resumed.

BOOK FIVE

One

The rich and powerful always think that they can create Arcadia. They think that they can impose it on the world. They think that they can re-create paradise within their terrestrial realms. It was one such attempt that the crew were visiting that day. And as if to underline the ambiguous impossibility of such ventures, a strange thing happened to them before they set out in the vans waiting to take them to the famed acres of Versailles.

They had met as arranged at the front of the hotel, and all were there except for Jim and Husk. A crowd of people streamed through the crew. Some confusion ensued. The crowd, tourists and city-dwellers, had surged at the crew from a direction no one could ascertain. And when the crowd passed, one of the crew members began shouting. It turned out to be Riley. She was hollering something in a mixture of Danish and bad French. She seemed quite unlike herself. The serenity that had embalmed her troubled nature had evaporated, and revealed strange torments within. The other crew members converged on her protectively. It wasn't long before the name Malasso was heard again, this time from Jute. The inscrutable Malasso had delivered another message.

In the midst of the confusion caused by the crowd, someone had slipped something into Riley's hand. At first, when she saw it, she thought she had been slashed with something fine and sharp like a razor. She felt the slicing of her palm, and it seemed that blood dripped down from her hand onto the pavement. That was why she screamed. But on further examination it turned out to be another red message, a message soaked in blood, or red ink. And as soon as she read the message, and crushed it in her palm, the blood or ink ran down her arm, red against her pale white flesh, causing everyone to gasp, as at a suicide.

She kept the message and its contents to herself, ran to the hotel, disappeared into the women's lavatory, stayed there a long time, and when she emerged her eyes were red, but her face was calm. The serenity that had taken quiet residence in her when she had vanished on the train and reappeared, was now quite gone. In its place was a nervous and twitching visage. She said nothing, averted her eyes, and got into the van.

In complete silence they travelled on to the earthly delights of a famous king.

Two

There is something about a sinister message received, a private sign, a personal future-reading, which when not shared awakens in others either a sense of doom or of awe. It was in this mixed mood that they travelled. When they arrived at Versailles they were struck by the grandeur of the place, by the balance and might of the architecture, by the great sprawling fields, by the tranquil spaces, and by the sheer scale and enormity of the buildings. There were tourists everywhere. They formed long queues all over the crowded courtyards.

Husk went all over, straining her poor French to the limit, trying to find their guide. It was a hot day. Children played in the great forecourt that enhanced the brilliance of the king's palace.

The rich and powerful always think that they can create Arcadia, and for the kings of France, Versailles was a terrestrial paradise. Its vast acreage, its fountains, its wonderful staircases, its grandeur and tranquillity, the openness of its grounds, with abundant space to ride horses, to play, to be free, to hold masques, outdoor dramas, massive festivities – all of it ought to have set the scene for great human happiness and contentment. It ought to have provided the background for noble productions of genius for the enrichment of the human race. It ought to have become one of those places out of which flow fountains of universal munificence. This was what the crew members sensed without knowing. As they toured the grounds with their guide they were each one of them struck by how beautiful it was and by how locked into itself its great beauty was. Jute found much to complain about in this, and was heard muttering about how useless great beauty can be.

At first Lao himself was puzzled. His feelings were too complex to be reduced to a single reaction. As they were taken through the little kingdom of the Sun King, Lao experienced an odd, incomplete intuition. He was overwhelmed with a reminder that at some moments the earth seemed like a fabulous stage set for an immortal drama, or initiation. The trees, the arbours, the orchards, the sweeping fields, the abundant heavens, all the astonishing colours of nature, the flowers, the hills, the lakes – it all seemed the most extraordinary setting for wonderful events, for the most fabulous adventures in living, for marvellous festivities of the human spirit. The perfect setting for humanity to perform the most amazing feats of history making, of self-overcoming, of transcending, of momentous 'becoming'. We have the setting, Lao was thinking, we have the consciousness, but the grand event, the luminous initiation, is missing. It seems we are not up to it. Here we have a world of legends, of pyramids, of oceans, of mountains, deserts, valleys, meadows, volcanoes, waterfalls, colours that bring tears to the eyes, we have trees and flowers and animals of unbelievable variety, we have civilisations vanished and civilisations that are here, we have a world shining with mysteries and terrors. The stage couldn't be better – and yet it seems we are not up to it. Our imagination is not commensurate with the splendour and potential of the stage provided. Our love is not commensurate with the possibilities of the world. It seems we are not up to the grandeur of the tremendous stage of nature, of the earth, of the universe. We are overwhelmed by the power, the vastness, and the unknowability of it all. Humanity suffers from a profound stage fright. Faced with the awesomeness of it all, before the marvellous setting fit for gods and monarchs of the mind, humanity is frigid. The most dramatic thing we've been able to do, it seems, with this setting fit for masters of the spirit, is wage war. There ought to be a creative equivalent of waging wars, something worthy of this masterpiece of creation, thought Lao, in a flash of incomplete illumination.

But Mistletoe merely gazed and stored away the sublimity of what she saw. She stored it in her soul, stored it away deep in her aesthetic spirit so she could draw upon it often in the difficult days that will inevitably come. Like gathering treasures within. Replenishing a place deep in the secret foundations of inspiration.

Jim, however, was so focused that he saw not much else but filming possibilities. Sam looked only for the most oblique and difficult shots to make all that beauty more human. Riley did her job, silently, with an odd quality of resignation on her face. And Husk busied herself everywhere, connecting strands, preparing the way, organising transport, losing herself utterly in work. It seemed she didn't dare allow herself to see the beauty all around for fear that it might make her weep for love's tender whispers and strolls, a love that was gone, devoured by just about everything. Never did beauty so threaten to make her so miserable.

Jim made Lao get on a tiny train in which sightseers journeyed round the extensive grounds of the palace. Lao was struck by the irony of having travelled to France on a train that sped on at two hundred miles an hour, when now he was on a little train that crawled at two miles an hour.

Filming was complicated. Sam was in his element. He went through much fine suffering to get to some private sense of artistic authenticity. Many trains were taken and gotten off and taken again before the shots were satisfactorily engrained with the mysterious existential quality that satisfied Sam.

'Suffering for art can become another kind of sentimentality,' Lao muttered now and again.

Sam, in fine form, was impervious.

And through it all Riley brooded on the message that had flowed like blood down her pale arm.

Three

All great spaces and mighty buildings hint at the possibility of happiness. They even inspire, for a moment, for the space of a lovely afternoon, the notion of happiness in visitors. Would that the perfection of palaces helped to inspire the perfection of human beings. Would that the cultivated acres created the conditions for the greatest cultivation of the human genius in all those that reside in them. Would that great architecture were the external sign of the greatness of those that dwell within.

But art is a dream of perfection. And the dream is always many realms away from the reality. Art is an indication of how balanced, how serene, how great, how beautiful we can be – an impossible indication. Civilisations are therefore measured by their dreams, by their aspirations in stone, in words, or paint, or marble. It is the artistic ideals of civilisations that signal where those civilisations hope the human spirit can go, how high it can ascend, into what deeds of astonishment it can flow. Art is the best selves of a people made manifest, one way or another. It is not their reality.

Arcadia can only come out of reality, not an ideal: that is the wonderful contradiction of it. Arcadia can only come out of deeds, not dreams, out of living, not dreaming: that is the strength of its enchantment. Arcadia is not a promise, nor a hope, nor an ideal embodied, nor cultivated acres. It is not in what is seen, but in what is created, evoked, found within.

Versailles is the dream, the reality of kings. It is terrestrial grandeur, a great space shaped and possessed under the stars. It is the embodiment of power, but not power itself. The embodiment of beauty, but not beauty itself. It is a mystery how much happiness it evokes in the ordinary visitors that throng its lakes and fields, and how little happiness it created in many of its inhabitants.

These were floating intuitions among the crew as they surveyed the landed dream of kings.

Four

After the first phases of filming the crew took a lunch break near the lake. All were struck by how fabulous the grounds were, how endless. The place seemed like a realm unto itself. Lao and Mistletoe listened to the rest of the crew as they expressed their delight or their dismay. Then, after a while, they decided to go for a turn together round the lake.

Mistletoe bought ice-creams and gave Lao his. Together they walked into the tender beauty of the golden sunlight. A clear wonderful happiness rose up in Mistletoe that afternoon. She was revisiting the scene of a childhood journey. And the child in her that delighted many years back at the splendour of the palace was still in delight now. The child that was happy, that played by the lake, and ate ice-cream under the loving supervision of her mother was awake and alive now. And her smile was a beautiful benediction to all who saw her. And her happiness made Lao happy.

They climbed one charming set of stone stairs and walked the length of the shimmering waters. They looked up towards another set of rising stairs of solid stone, and gazed on the geometric symmetry of the palace in the distance. And they marvelled at how architecture, if beautiful and balanced, is a sort of embodied happiness in space. It is joy made visible, a homeland of the dreaming self given concrete shape. It raises the spirits up towards its own noble dreaming and ideals. It seems to say to the viewer: 'I live in you. My genius rests in you because you have seen me thus. My proportions are in you because you feel them. My nobility is in you because you respond to it. There is nothing that you see in me, that you respond to in me, that isn't in you, slumbering. If I am great then I am a greatness that is sleeping in you. If I have something of the eternal then it is the eternal that lives and hides in you. Therefore when you look upon me and marvel, look upon yourself, and arise, and rise.'

Mistletoe heard the buildings and the spaces speaking thus, filling the air with silent hymns, and paeans, and poems of sensual and spiritual delight. The air was clear and warm, and gold was in all the spheres. Joy resided in every breath that was drawn in those happy moments above the lake. All around the green glowed, trees caught the light and became dark and ruby rich in their playful hidden green. How the colours played and danced on that radiant day. Beauty was in the air. The skin of the girls shone with delight and freshness. The spaces, cleansed and enriched with summer's ripening sensuality, made the women more amazing, and compacted into their future dreams some sort of enchantment without a name, or a place, or a land, detached from its origins, connected to the gentle breeze of eternity that makes all good dreams a glimpse of a forgotten Eden.

And when Lao and Mistletoe turned to face the lake, joy swooped down on them and linked their spirits to the hidden stars of heaven. And so gently did the light on the waters, stretching out in space, mirroring the wavy clouds and the broken heavens, so gently did the light on the waters steal away their hidden troubles that they were left weightless in wonder, afloat in delight.

The sense of wonder lasted long enough to be changed into something else. For Lao had heard much about the vanities of the Sun King, and about the mathematical symbolism of infinity that permeated the carousel.

Five

But it was only later, when Lao and Mistletoe decided to take separate journeys round the lake, to meet at the place where they had parted, that something monstrous began to speak through the vast project to conquer space and remake nature after a king's self image.

There was indeed something of the demiurge in the vanity of it all. The statues, the one hundred thousand and two hundred trees, the chariot rising from the lake, the unused fields, the buildings more amazing than functional, the complex mathematical computation of it all – the carousel devoured the nation's strength and finance. It had something of the mad divine fantasies of empire builders, mausoleum builders, constructors of gigantic monuments to the power of kings and emperors. Monuments that spoke of the ego, but not of the people.

As Lao walked alone and anticlockwise round the lake, and saw the rigidity of shaping nature to a fixed design, he found himself thinking of the secret meaning of things. Maybe, he thought, the grandiose designs of kings are meant to avert death, to temporise it, to delay it, to contain it, to defy it in their own deification. But in the strangest way he felt how much death spoke here through the great beauty of the place. Death spoke not through decay, but through the absence of freedom; and the happiness that he felt here had more to do with the sunlight on water, on the trees, on the grass, and on the wide open spaces. But death spoke from the design, from the attempt to create

Arcadia according to one's image and command. Death spoke through the geometry of it. Death spoke through the excess of symbolism. Death spoke through the labyrinths. Death spoke through the mathematics. And death sang through the sublime vanity of it all. And yet there was a strange breath of immortality in the air, a curious whiff of the stars...

Six

Lao had made his turn round the lake. It had taken an hour. But when he returned to where they had parted, Mistletoe wasn't there. He waited a while longer, and slowly a feeling of dread grew in him. Then, seeing the crew making signs to him that lunch break was over, and that filming was due to begin, he hurried off in the direction Mistletoe had taken, and went searching for her.

He looked for her through the labyrinths of the Sun King's fantasy. The light was so blinding that at one point he felt he was walking through mirrors. Near the fountain of Apollo he passed a theatrical troupe, dressed as cavaliers. They shouted words at him, and made signs which he couldn't understand. They ran in the opposite direction.

He rested near one of the gates of Hercules, and stared both ways, and his vision warped in the strange disappearing space of the water seeming to rise into the air like a lifting illusion of a road in a shimmering desert oasis. He shut his eyes. Then he went among the trees. There, a group of harlequins, singing German drinking songs, danced past him, and laughed at his bewilderment. Then he heard voices singing beautifully all around him, with no one in sight. Feeling that the heat and the cold mystery of the place were beginning to overwhelm him, he hurried back in the direction of the café where the crew would be waiting. But he got lost, and couldn't find his way.

He lay near the pool of Latona and fell into an oblique

mathematical reverie, in which Mistletoe stood over him, with the sun framing her head. She led him into a chariot and they rode over the points of perspectives on a road that was composed entirely of sun rays. And as they rode, Mistletoe began reciting Virgil's famous fourth eclogue over his sleeping form while the constellations whirled above him, and while the abyss swirled below. And then, suddenly, he found himself in a realm, alone with Mistletoe, where they wandered in a glass labyrinth. They came to a room, a vast room, where beings dwelt who were old men and young men, old women and young women. They all had branches of trees growing out of their human heads, and they were dying. The youngest of them came to Lao and Mistletoe, and said:

'We are the sons and daughters of the great god Pan, and we are dying. We are the last of the great god's offspring. There used to be millions of us all over the earth. We were worshipped and loved. We were treated with reverence and we blessed the earth with munificence and fruits and food and happy things. But now we are dying. The world has lost the meaning of the infinite, and the finite is without sustenance. What you see is held up by what you do not see. The visible is sustained by the invisible. You depend on us, and we on you. Therefore, if you can, you must help us, or there will be no future left for you all to enjoy.'

And Lao said:

'How can we help?'

And one of the beautiful daughters of Pan came forward and said:

'Restore us to our place. Lead us out of this dying space. Turn your prayers into deeds. Do things that are possible. Don't get lost in your search for ideals. Listen to the inscription. Follow the guide of your heart. Link hands and bring nature back to the centre. Let the infinite speak in your smallest deeds of love. Life has no greater meaning than to turn into the flowers of love. That way death gives off light, and even hell is averted.'

Then Mistletoe spoke.

'We must do something,' she said. 'We must begin now. We must lead them out of their dying place. We must pass on the word. We must organise and prepare for a new earth. The old earth is dying.'

Seven

And together, they began to act, to organise. And the sons and daughters of Pan followed them into the wider spaces of the world where they could bloom again, and freshen humanity. And they did this while listening to one of the daughters of Pan singing magic lines from Virgil's fourth eclogue under the sunlight of the last years of the old earth. And when the new earth dawned, with the sweetest spring in the air, after the darkest winter, the world began to thrive again, and to shine with a new radiance.

And Lao woke up suddenly under the beech tree where he had lain. He found Mistletoe standing over him, singing a French song from her childhood. In a flash he remembered something from his dream which he wasn't aware of at the time, and which troubled him. During the great time of change, as they passed from the dark place into the intermediate place of the long years, they crossed a place called the mirrors of eternity. And Lao had gasped in surprise when he saw in his dream that Mistletoe had branches coming out of her head. Then he realised what it was he had always found so mysterious about her, what he found so unfathomable. And he understood why it seemed so natural that she was with him on this quest for the Arcadian dream. As he awoke now and saw her head framed by the branches of distant trees, he said:

'Ah, my dear sweet Mistletoe, I should have guessed that you are one of the daughters of Pan.'

And he told her of his dream. And she crouched next to him, and said:

'That was my dream. That was a dream I told you about, six months ago.'

After thinking a while, he said:

'That is true. But I only understand it now that I have had the dream myself. I understand your serenity and your anxiety better now. Let's be getting back. The crew must be going crazy worrying about us.'

She helped him up. And hurrying without haste, they walked alongside the great lake, towards the palace. They barely glanced at the statue of Enceladus in the clear mirror of the water.

And as they walked alongside the lake – the length of water that stretched to a very human termination – Lao had the feeling that the smooth surface of the water was a parallel road on which invisible beings played, on which magic notions wandered off into a flawed human infinity.

Eight

Jim was upset with Lao when he finally got to the café. The crew had been waiting impatiently. Lao felt like a child that had done something both delightful and naughty. He'd been away so long that the crew had started to worry about him and Jim in particular feared that something unthinkable had happened. Jim was more upset because he was more concerned. Lao was very touched by this and felt it necessary to elaborate a genuine apology which, coming from him, surprised everyone and earned him instant forgiveness.

As the crew got into the van that was to take them to the next point of their filming, commotion was stirring in the great lake. A young anarchist had scrambled in and, with seven balloons in one hand, was shouting:

'Beware! Beware! Beware of this false paradise!'

Crowds gathered. Tourists, thinking it part of the attraction, a piece of French drama, began taking pictures. Someone sent for the police. The young man went on:

'Beware! Hell hides in all this beauty! Death grows in this sublimity! Don't let grandeur fool you! The blood of the people boils under all this perfection. This place is built with corpses, and this lake shines with tears! Rip it all down! And make the small places beautiful! Beware! Don't be seduced by all this purity, this glamour! Make your lives your special places, and leave these lies to fools...'

And as the van pulled away, Lao saw the attendants storm the lake and try to drag the young anarchist back onto land. They soon grabbed hold of him. At that very moment he released his seven balloons. And all seven balloons, red and gold on that golden day, drifted over the terrestrial paradise of kings, and disappeared into the surrounding worlds.

Soon the bus had turned a corner, and the scene had vanished. Something in their journey was underlined. No one spoke till they got to their next destination.

Nine

The rich and powerful try to create Arcadia and only end up constructing a labyrinth. They try to shape a paradise and end up as prisoners. To those with a metaphysical take on history, the Sun King was a prisoner of infinity. To others a prisoner of unreality.

As they drove in silence deeper into the grounds of Versailles, Lao read the notes that Husk had prepared for their next encounter.

'The court of Versailles was not everyone's idea of paradise. Marie Antoinette, the wife of Louis XVI, preferred a constructed village, with goats and sheep, at the far corner of the rolling acres of the palace. How much like the traditional condition of things: behold the man's possessions, his 100,200 trees, his 160 million flowers, his 43 kilometres of streets, his canal, his lakes, his châteaux, fountains, servants, his innumerable houses and their numberless rooms and lavatories everywhere. And the woman, the queen, has only a little patch, far away, to call her own. She had only a constructed little village, to call her own. It is just over a mile away from the palace. A little hamlet with its own farm, pond, and mill.'

The crew spilled out of the bus and gazed upon the charming hamlet which a queen had created for her own pleasure. It could have been a quaint fairy-tale village, and had much of the air of little Swiss towns, or the little villages that girls have in their picture books. A doll's village, with a lake, a château, a mill and pond, shepherds' huts, and an abundance of plants and flowers and its own woods. There was a garden house and a house for the policeman. There was a beautiful little tower, and a theatre where comedies were staged. There was also a house for the poor, beautifully thatched with grass.

The curator of the preserved hamlet, a Monsieur Torraban, led the crew round the infamous extravagance of the Petit Trianon. He showed them the paddock where the cows and sheep were kept. He was generally enthusiastic when speaking in French. And he seemed to have a charming effect on Husk. She coloured often and perked up in his company. She seemed, for a while, to have forgotten that she was heartbroken. And when she announced to Jim an amusing forthcoming problem to do with the interview, she was almost girlish.

Monsieur Torraban, it seemed, had spoken perfectly acceptable English in their previous discussions, but when it came to the moment of the interview he panicked. He refused to speak anything but French and was as intractable as a mule. Monsieur Torraban kept disappearing during the linguistic negotiations and each time he returned he seemed more stressed and more drunken than before. By the time of the interview itself, he was positively refractory.

At this point Lao came forward, told Sam to start filming, and the whole interview was plunged into a strange transaction of languages. In the end Lao forced the poor distraught fellow to speak in his pretty ropy English as it was marginally better than Lao's threadbare French.

Their conversation, which lasted hours, and needed many disappearances on Monsieur Torraban's part, reduced the entire crew to stitches of laughter. But what emerged was something charming and sad.

Ten

While there was famine and misery in the land, while the poor stewed in diseases and hunger, while the spirit of revolution grew fat, Marie Antoinette instigated the creation of the hamlet and went there to escape the rigidity of court life and to indulge her fantasies. She went there to be free. It was her Arcadia. She had read Rousseau, had been influenced by his ideal of going back to nature, and attempted to put it into practice. Also she longed for the simplicity of her childhood in Austria. Away from the splendid artificiality of court life in Versailles, she created an artificial oasis.

And when she came here, with her chosen ones and attendants, it wasn't to be a queen, but a shepherdess. She wanted the place to be as authentic as possible. When she arrived she would change into the costume of a shepherdess and play at living the simple life. Her sheep were beribboned with silk, her cows were aristocratic, the trees and rocks were tricked with hand-laid moss, and her shepherds and milkmaids wore fake peasant outfits. She fished sea bass from the lake, and acted in plays with her friends, composed operettas and sang in the little theatre. Some say she even milked the cows herself, though this is doubted. The hamlet was her dream of freedom.

One fascinating thing was that though there was a twin château in the hamlet for the king, he never went there at all. And, most telling of all, the splendid mill was nothing but a beautiful façade, a stage effect. The mill was pure decoration, there only for the effect of beauty. The mill-house had tiny rooms that had never been used for anything, and never could be, like rooms in a doll's house. Inside the mill-house, there was nothing.

The queen came to the hamlet on horseback, played and picked flowers in her Arcadia, and left. She never spent the night there. By day it was enchanting, by night deserted.

Meanwhile, there was famine in the land. Meanwhile, she was infuriating the French with scandals, ignoring the courtiers, and contemptuous of the poor. Meanwhile, her Arcadia concealed from her the guillotine that would chop off her head.

Eleven

Hours passed. The afternoon's blaze settled gently into the cool breeze of early evening. After filming was finished, all the crew members wandered around the pleasant conceit of the queen's private playground. Beyond, where the shadows of the trees were lengthening on the grass, was the terrain that some would have thought an earthly paradise, a place where anyone could be happy, could create, could think noble thoughts and plant them in the world.

And as they wandered about the hamlet they each had different incomplete intuitions about the Arcadias of the rich and powerful, intuitions that drifted in the breeze with the fragrance of roses.

Twelve

Jim's Intuition

Immensity of the land
And spaces of the sun.
They slept too long in paradise
And ended up in prison.

Thirteen

Propr's Intuition

and then because she so ignored the cries of the people, lost as she was in her Arcadia, she was eventually guillotined.

Arcadia can become a hiding place from reality. It can become a deafness and a cruelty and an indifference to suffering.

They create their Arcadia and hide from the evils of the world and Arcadia becomes a kind of evil too. And then it feeds the monster that will eventually devour them.

Arcadia cannot be a denial of reality, for reality cannot be denied.

It is not a place or dream to hide in. It cannot protect you from truth, or injustice, or poverty.

It can only delay your death by the truth you don't face.

Arcadia ought to help us be more candid.

Fourteen

Mistletoe's Intuition

Hades dwells in false Arcadias. Their effect is a cold delightful decoration. Lifeless, false Arcadias don't have the power of death.

Arcadia charms death. And death makes Arcadia enchanting, eternally haunting. Death makes Arcadia immortal.

And so, wherever there is a true Arcadia, there is the breath of immortality, sweetened by the flowers of mortal things.

Arcadia is the chiaroscuro of the mortal and the immortal, of happiness and death, of eternity and transience, beauty and the grave.

Fifteen

Jute's Intuition

tyrants and dictators all had their Arcadias to cleanse their souls of the brutalities they had unleashed.

The makers of the Holocaust wanted to create vast shining Arcadias that masked the incredible evils that they had wrought in daylight.

Such vast visible Arcadias hint at vast hidden evils and injustices.

They are an affront to a world reeking with suffering and starvation, the poor, the imprisoned, the refugees, the oppressed.

The immense Arcadias of the powerful are suspect; they have an ambivalent astonishment.

Sixteen

And as the film crew climbed into their van, and got lost several times trying to get out of the vast grounds of Versailles, they were silent, and a little depressed.

They had lived through a wonderful day. The weather had been perfect, the sunlight blessed. The sign of the great stairs, the dreaming lake, and the rich fountains was still shimmering in their minds. They had been touched by the lovely space of l'Hameau, but there was still this sadness. It fell with the sense of the journeys still to be undertaken before Arcadia can be glimpsed. But it fell more with the subliminal realisation that with all the money in the world, all the power in the world, all the land, the fame, the will, the dream, the desire and the genius, Arcadia could not be created by human will or hand on earth. It can only be revealed, found, stumbled upon, discovered.

But their sadness came more from the fact that they had just passed into and emerged from one of the saddest things of all: a false Arcadia amidst splendour and glory.

It is better to endure the nakedness of despair than the emptiness of a fake Arcadia.

But the charm of the false Arcadia lingers, and deepens the ache for the real.

The crew's sadness was that ache for the real, for the authentic enchantment.

PART THREE

BOOK SIX

BOOK SIX

One

Intuitions before Dreaming (1)

If music was born out of grief, painting was born out of transience within an immortal universe. Painting is the charmed presence of what will no longer be there. An enchanted absence, a visible dream, a parallel universe, defying death, underlining life's brevity.

Painting is the meaning of humanity in a visible moment. It is the parable without text, the mystery without ritual. Painting is a hint of the intuition of the gods. It is spying on an immortal pageant. It is seeing the compressed history of humanity through the camera obscura of heaven. It is the frozen music of time's justice and injustice. It is a vision of life from Hades enchanted. It is the secret history of light, the psychodrama of colour, the moment in a mind, the moment in a song.

Painting is what those in the Underworld remember. It is how the dead dream. It is how the enigma of time manifests itself on the cyclorama of matter. Painting is the magic riddle of mortality. It is the longing for the eternal, the happiness of the transient, the enigma of creation, the home of the heart, the fountain where loss is soothed. It is the eternal future, for painting is never in the past tense, only in the ever flowing present tense, an eternal now, a never-ending summer, a life always living, a moment never ceasing.

Painting is water, air, fire, earth, dream, but it is never death. Painting is life, life smiling at death with light as its secret.

Painting is Narcissus surprised. Painting is secret structures, harmonies, balance, chaos, force-fields, philosophy, patience, rhythm, wit, sadness, delight, tragedy. Painting is the invisible made visible, the allegory of unseen things, the resting place of a visual thought, eternal youth. Painting even when it decays is like a dream vanishing.

Painting is the Turin shroud, the manifestation of the hidden avatar on white cloth.

When paintings die, they go back to God's mind.

Two

Intuitions before Dreaming (2)

Painting is an inscription on the flesh of time. An invocation of colours. Painting is a raising from the dead, a resurrection, a transmogrification, a transmutation. Painting is the triumph of plants and minerals and animal hair. It is soul dancing to soul.

Painting is the still life of God's mind. It is the heaven of remembered things, the hell of forgotten things. It is the destiny of legend, the dream of a faun and all legendary beings. It is legend frozen, memory's homeland.

Painting is the nightmare of the devil. Codes in colours and shapes. It is the yearning of all things to live and persist in memory. Painting is the only mortal space where angels dwell in stillness. It is meditation with eyes wide open, contemplation with the mind's eyes focused on enigmas. It is visualisation materialised. The mind's strength and grace trembling in space. The unending lesson of the ascending spirit.

Painting is the tentative deciphering of destiny, the visual haiku of human history, musings of life in deep dimensions. Painting is illusion impacting on the real, becoming the real, insisting on its ability to be more real than that which has vanished. Painting is human love transcending human forgetfulness. It is mortality staring at itself in the evanescent mirror of immortality. It is spaces dancing, dimensions interacting, realms interpenetrating, time zones colliding, eliding, harmonising.

Painting is the shaman's mirror, the warrior's truest shield, the healer's armour against fate and tragedy. The celebration of light.

Painting is the weapon the wise use against vicissitude. It will one day heal profound sicknesses of body, mind, and spirit. It is the technology of the wise primitive, the science and medicine of the forgotten ancients.

Three

Intuitions before Dreaming (3)

Painting is the magic charm that nature herself has invented in all things that breathe and move and that don't breathe and don't move. There is healing in it. There is wisdom in it. There is hope in it. And there is unfathomed power in its undiscovered potentials.

Painting is one of the earliest tools of survival. You painted a thing first then you made it manifest later, you made it happen, you made it real. There is painting of the mind, where you first create the complete form of a thing or dream or desire and feed it deep into the spirit's factory for the production of reality. Painting is the mirror of healing, the base of creativity, the springboard of materialisation.

Those who can't paint in the mind can never create useful power in the world. Those who can't paint in the spirit can never create happiness or overcome obstacles in life. Painting is the mathematics of making things possible. It is planting notions in the subconscious through the allure or disturbance of the eyes.

Great paintings transcend the eyes and, through other agencies, can be transmitted from soul to soul. All dreamers are spirit painters. All dreams are paintings. All spirit painters are world remakers. Painting is the refresher of love, the aider of love, the incarnation of loving.

Painting is time multiplied by light. It is the sweet sister of beauty, the ambiguous sister of history, the still life of humanity.

Painting is where the dead sleep, is where the labyrinth is decoded. It is the secret film of the gods, the ecstasy of dyes, the paradigm of better ways of being.

Painting is the illuminated record book of invisible realms seen in glimpses. Intimations of reincarnation. Akashic stillpoints. Painting is indeed one of the places where Hades is averted. It is the hint of a sort of immortality within. It comes from the same place inside us where gods are born.

Painting is one of the most mysterious metaphors of Arcadia.

Four

That night, after the crew had returned to Paris, they had an early dinner and, too tired to discuss anything, went to bed early.

Each in their own way had been enchanted and disturbed by the day's events.

Each was troubled and fascinated by what they would discover the next day.

They were all due to film in the Louvre.

They were all acquainted with the mysterious painting that was at the centre of their visit to Paris, at the centre, even, of their ambiguous journey.

They had all postponed thinking about the painting, for they had other things to trouble them, to engage their minds.

No more messages had been received from the insidious manifestations of Malasso.

Everything was still more or less on schedule.

Jim worried most when everything was going well; he always felt it was fate's way of seducing him into unwatchfulness and then pouncing on him with unsuspected disasters.

He slept badly.

They all slept badly.

The pressure of future enigmas weighed on their sleeping forms.

Five

Mistletoe's Dream

She was a daughter of Pan and had been wandering in a landscape of trees and flowers. The air was sweetened with amaranth. There were acorns on the grass. A chain of ochre mountains ranged all around her, bare and stark and oddly beautiful. She knew that the mountains were the forms of sleeping gods, the ancient forgotten gods.

It was a brilliant day. The sun was benevolent in its universal golden splendour. There were a few lovely clouds, and within one of the clouds was the exact form of an angel in flight.

She was in the homeland of human happiness. She was happy, and had been eternally happy, like a fortunate child. She had known no suffering and had always been surrounded with love.

But as she wandered in this realm of happiness she came upon three men who stood puzzled before a gigantic tomb.

The men were shepherds.

She had never seen them before.

They were grizzled, but seemed harmless.

On the enormous tomb there was an inscription, which read: ET IN ARCADIA EGO.

She was one of the daughters of Pan, and yet the inscription troubled her. The men fretted over the inscription and kept pointing at it, while their shadows took on sinister shapes.

She noticed that the man who pointed most ardently at the word ARCADIA had formed the shadow of a man with a scythe.

This troubled her more.

They asked her about the tomb.

But she had never seen a tomb before. They explained what it was. She turned pale.

They contemplated the inscription and the mystery of the tomb till the shadows grew shorter and stranger on the wind-quivering grass. The world had darkened into tones of a deep bright sombre beauty.

Sadness seemed to be leaking into the happy kingdom of the earth.

And when she left the men, who remained discussing the inscription for what seemed like the rest of their lives, she was never quite so happy again.

And her life now seemed as a bright golden dream of ambiguities when she woke up in the dark.

Six

Jim's Nightmare

He was in a gigantic tomb in which existed all the happiness of the world. He tried to tell travellers on earth of this happiness but all he ended doing was becoming an inscription which no one could decode, which no one cared about – an inscription in a place of immortal bliss, in a land that used to be called Eden, but which was renamed Arcadia, and it was all the lands of the earth.

Seven

The Mystery of the Invisible Third Man

And the secret of the treasure they were unknowingly seeking was in the painting. Jim couldn't find it. But they filmed it, and they all saw it without recognising what they saw.

Three men stood at a distance while they filmed. Two of the men were museum workers. But the third man came to them and, addressing Lao, said:

'The Treasure map is there, in that painting. Follow the map carefully. Follow it truthfully, for the map is in you. Eat the inscription. Eat it over and over again when you are hungry. But don't eat the acorns. The Oak Tree is sacred, and is your secret symbol. Avoid the evil shade. Don't forget that the landscape is greater than the tomb. Death is merely Time's inscription, a beautiful absence. Don't dwell too long in Arcadia. This is fatal. For if you dwell too long there, you become the tomb, and your life its inscription. Arcadia looks backward. There is a great and mysterious beauty in this, a haunting wisdom. But look forward. Go forward. Come down from the mountain. Return to the Valley. And begin again. There you will find the Treasure, not at the end, but at the beginning.'

And then the eloquent third man turned and left the great hall of the museum. And when Lao asked everyone who he was, nobody could say, nobody knew, because nobody had seen him.

And Lao puzzled over this third man even when he awoke.

Eight

As You Don't Like It

and Propr found himself in the forest of Arden, among exiled kings and their courtiers, among lovers and melancholy scholars. And among them he was a farmer.

The women were beautiful and scented the air with wit. The men were exiled but mostly happy. They were all happy except him. And one of the exiled kings came up to him and said:

'My dear Propr, you do not like happiness, you are suspicious of pleasures, you think leisure a waste of time, and you frown on us kings who are exiled and ought to be miserable and yet we seem to be happier than we ever were in our carefree youth. But being a king is not everything. Being human is. The days on this earth are but the shortening shadow of the elm when night dissolves it into darkness, wherein no man can see without aid of light. Those who walk their days on the earth but never sing, never laugh, never caper, are but those who have lived with their feet only, but not their hearts. For life is part walking, part singing. It is a walking part, a walk-on role. And remember that the great poet Virgil said: "Singing makes the going easier". We are happy here in the forest of Arden, living under the branches and the stars, rediscovering the pleasures of comradeship and wine, learning how to be free again without grandeur. And when we recover our kingdom again, which we will, we might be better kings for having been happier, and the land will be better too. You are like us. You are a king disguised as a farmer. But when you frown you make your animals nervous. Free your moustache, and laugh a little. They say that laughter makes death wait for another day. You see, my dear grim Propr, Arden is the school where nature teaches us simplicity. Join us in our revels, for we will not be here long, and then the walking continues all the way to the famous tomb that speaks in Latin.'

And Propr lowered his moustache and smiled and danced through the night with the exiled kings in his beloved forest of Arden.

Nine

Love's Labour Redeemed

and a man came to Husk in a rocky region where she was waiting under a beech tree and said:

'What does it matter that love is lost? Love is a song that trembles in the air and is caught by another. Love is a sweet melody that haunts those that like your singing. Let it go, and it will come again in another form. If you don't let it go, it can never return, for a vessel that is full cannot be filled. But a vessel that is empty can be filled with rich new wine that you have never tasted before. And the new wine doesn't destroy the memory of the old, but enriches your palate and your sense of having lived much. Unused palates don't know good wine from bad. So, my weeping dear, come with me on the adventures across these mountains and let us both sing of our lovely loves lost that will come again from our singing. If you have emptied yourself in rich loving you will be ready for richer loving still. For loving is one of the most beautiful labours that ever the heart invented. But what does the labour create, what does it do? Does it make you rich, does it farm your lands, does it make a painting, does it make you famous, does it make you beautiful? It does all these things, but it does something better still – it makes a life, it sweetens a road travelled, it charms time, and gives us much to think about when the journey is ended. Yes, my dear, loving makes a life, it makes a melody of a life, which the soul goes on singing long after the sun has set. So let us go, singing of our love, and not be afraid that we have lost it, but glad that we once were loved, and once were happy. For, what with living and dying, our happiness will prove to be the brightest place in the painting. Let's leave this shade, and set out for the festivities, where we are young again.'

And Husk followed the stranger into the landscapes, away from the rocky regions where she had been wailing.

Ten

Riley's Regret

and Riley found herself among circus folk, wandering on a long road between cities, with Harlequin at her side.

She had no idea where she was going.

It was a beautiful day, and the sunlight seemed to radiate not from the sky, but upwards out of the earth, from the plants, from the hills, and from the lakes along the great road.

Harlequin was thin and handsome, quirky and prankish, and silent. He spoke to her in silence, with his expressive face.

She travelled with the circus folk and before they got to the city where they were due to be performing, she met a young man by the roadside, fell into a conversation, and together they went off to explore the villages. Before she knew it she had lost contact with her friends, the mute circus folk.

The dream jumped forward, and she was on the road again, another road, with the circus folk, and with Harlequin silent at her side.

Soon a pattern emerged in the dream which frustrated her. She seemed to be with her circus friends only between cities. And she always got distracted by some exciting thing or other before they arrived at the city where they were due to perform. And so she always lost contact with them and never got to join them in their fabulous performances to huge crowds.

She only ever met her circus friends again between cities, on the long road, with Harlequin telling of their wonderful adventures and passions in his expressive silence.

Eleven

Journey with Camels

and Sam always found himself journeying through a desert with camels that wouldn't let him ride on them.

And throughout the long trek, and the great thirst, and the sun beating down like a blacksmith's hammer on anvils, all he could think of was how to film the world from the back of a camel.

He spent the journey filming the sameness of the desert dunes and the expanse of sand and the storms and the unchanging bronze dream of the horizon.

And there was no one else in the whole world but the camels.

And after a long time walking on the shifting sands, he spied a distant oasis, and his heart leapt with joy. But the camels were not interested in the oasis and they travelled away from it. Sam was torn between the camels and the oasis, and couldn't decide between them.

Eventually he chose to follow the camels, and then he turned back again and went towards the oasis, and then turned again towards the departing camels, till the sandstorms came and obliterated the world at dawn.

Twelve

The Silence of Mothers

and Jute was in winter, with ice all around, under a darkening sky. Mozartian flute music sounded from far away in the distant festivities.

Jute was in winter. Her heart was cold. Her hands were freezing. But she sensed that there was a wonderful party going on all over the world. Only she could not get to the party because she was looking for her mother.

She was looking for her mother in the winter of her being and could not find her. And the winter grew worse while the beautiful music grew more haunting from the increasing distance.

Soon Jute found herself a prisoner in the block of ice of her own being. She had become the block of ice. And the party and the music were her mother.

Her mother was speaking to her from outside the ice but Jute could not hear because her ears were frozen.

After a while her mother stopped speaking and stood in her own splendid sunlight.

She looked at her daughter, silent in the encasement of ice.

And all around spring was in the air, and there was music and dancing at the fair on the happy green.

Thirteen

And so it was that they, each with their dreams still unresolved within them, arrived at the Louvre on a blessed day in September. They were all quieter than normal and were subdued the way people are when enrapt within a puzzle.

There was gaiety outside the Louvre. Lovers sat on the edge of the glass pyramid, and on the margin of the flowing waters, with the sunlight casting a lovely spell on the world.

The charmed open spaces and the sunlight on the splendid palace ought to have lifted the spirits of the crew. But each was enfolded, in-turned, uncommunicative. They each did the work they were meant to do, but without inspiration.

They were met by museum officials and led in through the back way, past the security checks. They were led down polished stone stairs and complicated corridors with Egyptian statues and sphinxes and walls with hieroglyphs; they passed through long rooms with prehistoric moulds and monoliths, with Iberian sculptings, African figures, ibexes in stone, idols in bronze.

Through many corridors and crypts were they led, through what seemed like underground routes and tunnels, through darkened places, emerging again within halls, ascending in lifts.

They journeyed through a universe of paintings, and were regarded by figures on walls in open-eyed dreams, who stared at them the way people do in a room when a stranger enters and disrupts a conversation.

For the first time Lao became conscious that paintings are living things. He became aware that figures within great paintings live and breathe and bustle and carry on their normal busy comic or tragic transactions away from human gaze. But when humans appear they stop and freeze, as if in a game, trying to behave as though they weren't real.

Lao and Mistletoe exchanged a glance. They knew at once that paintings can be intruded upon. That paintings have a secret life. That they have a secret world of dramas. That paintings contemplate themselves and that the crew was interrupting their contemplation, their activities, and their dreams.

Mistletoe could sense the figures in the paintings waiting for the crew to pass on, to leave them alone. And as the crew entered each room they could feel this unbroken breathing, this sudden stopping of all activity, like children who are up to some mischief ceasing their suspicious play when their parents suddenly appear in the doorway.

It was Tuesday, and the museum was closed to the public, and the air was pristine and fresh with the breathing of paintings, with the breathing of angels and villains, of heroes and gods, of beautiful women and goddesses.

The sunlight of fresher worlds, distant worlds, was present and alive and shining forth its radiance into the stillness of the rooms, filling the spaces with other times, sending the passing film crew into other time zones, making other time realms present, removing them from a day in September to a timeless space where dreams are more real than things.

And they journeyed forth, led by the museum guide, into the great labyrinth of the Louvre. They wandered through dreams materialised in the air, troubled by the gaze of horses, or a murder witnessed, or a suicide enacted, in silence, alone. They were perturbed by glimpses of ravished women, amazed by an intense

Napoleon on his wild horse, and astonished by the serenity of a betrayed Christ.

On and on through the swirling spaces they went, tiptoeing so as not to disturb the tranquillity of paintings, silent so as not to alarm the settled dew of stillness.

Fourteen

Their complicated journey through the crypts and labyrinths of the Louvre was fitting. Their main reason for being in Paris was to see not only one of the most enigmatic paintings in the world, but also one of the most important icons of the Arcadian legend.

Fifteen

There is a mood in which all great things must be appreciated. This mood can be induced through surprise, through indirection, through the tangential, by accident, by serendipity. It can be induced through complete ignorance, or by strong contrast, or by long complicated routes that lead you into the mind's openness to illumination. This mood can be brought on through the relentless pressure of reverential whispers hints rumours praise controversy negativity hostility or the unaccountable silence that surrounds an achievement that no one is as yet willing to face. Like the silence around a strange mountain that no one suspects is there.

In what other ways can this mood be created? Through the elaborate journey of a great accomplishment in the byways and highways of thought and tradition, through its sheer unavoidability, through the ways in which an aspect of important thought is impossible without confronting or facing it. Or through the way it haunts you, or haunts others, haunts those you respect and revere, through its unfathomability, its unavailability, its unapproachability, its elusiveness, its overwhelming and mysterious fame, the persistence of its legend, or simply through the ways in which it confronts you at every turn, like a disturbing figure in a dream who appears at the end of every road you take to avoid a confrontation. Whatever you do they have already worked on you, and haven't finished yet. But great achievements can not properly be approached ordinarily.

There ought to be a ritual of encounter with all noble and amazing things. And so it proved to be with the crew as they entered the beautifully lit hall, after so many twists and turns through all kinds of spaces in the empty museum of one of the world's greatest collections of art.

Tuesday was the best day to film. The emptiness, the stillness, the silence of the place were spooky, and induced an air of mystery, of a ritual encounter.

Without knowing it for a long time afterwards, how were the crew to realise that it wasn't a painting they were about to encounter, but themselves and their unclear and enigmatic place in the universe, within the shining sphere of life?

Sixteen

And when they entered the hall and encountered the painting it was with a sense of anticlimax. Oh, the mystery of all deservedly famous achievements! How they always seem smaller than their fame suggests! How it is that they do not perform instant miracles on the first encounter! That they don't make the senses jump, and don't burst into song like the ancient oracles when the mood of Apollo had seized their hidden sibyls!

Deservedly famous achievements are always smaller than their fame, and vaster. Upon greater study and immersion into their powers they always seem to be even more famous than they at first appeared. So it was when the crew first saw Poussin's *Les Bergers d'Arcadie.*

Seventeen

This painting is the epitome and the finest realisation of the Arcadian notion in art. It contains its beauty and mystery, its simplicity and its complexity, its hope and its despair, its power and its humility.

But above all, it is an open painting, impossible to decipher completely, a true enigma of the illuminati, a visual koan, a perpetual question, and a perpetual quest.

It gives no answers. But it gives the code for continual development in living, and in thinking. It is a nightmare to those who seek, and a preparatory school for those who find.

It fills you with peace. But within that peace it plants the seeds of restlessness, of unease, of subtle disturbance, like a meaningful dream not fully understood, filling your waking hours with question marks.

Eighteen

What is this painting? Is it a monster, a sphinx, a riddle, a mental labyrinth, the resting point of an idea that has travelled thousands of years in the mind of humanity, or a secret guide to the future?

Is it in fact a painting, or is it one of those things that transcend art, transcend their form, a question that immortality poses to mortality?

Nineteen

The painting appears simple. Three shepherds and a shepherdess in front of a tomb. The tomb is in a rocky landscape with a few trees. The four figures are reading the inscription on the tomb, and they appear to be trying to decipher it. The shepherdess stands slightly aloof from their puzzlement.

It is a beautiful painting, but the beauty does not reside in the landscape, which is rocky and mostly bare. The beauty is in the structure, the colours, the harmony of the lines of force in the painting, and in its mood.

At the centre of the painting is the tomb. And at the centre of the tomb is the inscription: Et in Arcadia Ego. Those four words are among the most debated in the history of art, the most enigmatic, puzzling, mysterious, and endless.

'I too have lived in Arcadia', the inscription reads. Who is the 'I'? Is it Death? Is it the one who died? There is no name on the tomb. So it can't be the one who is buried in it. The tomb itself seems to be the 'I'; or the unnamed dead within it. This unnaming makes it all of us, therefore it might be anyone who has died. They too have been in Arcadia. They too have lived. And now they are dead. We who look upon the painting are implicated. We stand with the shepherds. We too are in Arcadia. We are alive. We too will...

But if the tomb itself is the one that speaks its own inscription then it is saying that Death too has been in Arcadia, and is still there, in the form of the monumental tomb.

Like a silent explosion, a quiet inner revolution, a provocation to enlightenment, a ticking time bomb of illumination planted right in the midst of life's splendours, it is impossible for an intelligent human being to see this painting, to think about it, and to live the same way they lived before.

Twenty

Many things in the painting have puzzled commentators since the seventeenth century. The kneeling shepherd points at the word 'Arcadia' in the inscription – which is like pointing out the name on a map of the place in which you are looking at the map. Which is to say here, or 'Here'; or 'Now'.

So the inscription says: 'I too have been here', or 'I too have been in now'. Death too is here. Death too is now. Death lives concurrent with life; the two streams flow side by side, and sometimes intersect. Or Death is in life, not separate from it, but part of it, the way a capital city is part of a country, but is not the country.

The other puzzling thing is that the shepherd who points forms the shape of a man with a scythe in his shadow. The symbol of death. And so Arcadia and death are inextricably intertwined. Immortality and death are conjoined. Beauty and death are linked, happiness and death are coupled.

Twenty-one

This is the painting that the crew gathered round as they awaited the arrival of the museum director. And as they stared at it, seeing it and not seeing it, as they thought about what they thought they saw, as they discussed it, they were all changed by it, each in their own unique way.

But it was Lao who was most affected by the painting, because of his earlier confrontation, and because of what he had been told about the inscription. The message that had been sleeping within him since the beginning of the journey now awoke and sprang into life.

He wondered what warnings, what omens, the inscription was meant to signify to him personally. What did he have to beware of in those harmless lethal words? But he had hardly begun to think through the strange stirrings of his thoughts and his unease, when the director of the museum made his appearance, and filming began.

Twenty-two

And as the crew set up their equipment, took sound levels and light measurements, Lao found himself thinking not of the inscription as such, but of the journey of an idea through time. He was thinking about the journey of an idea from a real place to a poem; from the real Arkadia in the Peloponnese to the idyllic and pastoral poems of the Greek poet Theocritus, and from Theocritus to Virgil.

Virgil refined the pastoral form, and raised the potent beauty and ambiguity of the Arcadian notion till it became, in his *Eclogues*, a landscape of shepherds, a refuge for exiles, a place of disordered passions, a place of dispossession, a realm of love poetry, of singing matches, of an encounter with the tomb of the famous and beautiful Daphnis. It also became a setting for one of the most mysterious and messianic poems in literature, a terrain for the celebration of a god, a territory for the praise of the powerful, and a place of departure.

In short, Virgil transformed Arcadia into a landscape of the human spirit, where love, history, politics, religion, work, poetry, and power converge and live. With Virgil, Arcadia became the seed of an ideal, a dream, and a lyric meditation on the mystery of creation and creativity.

Twenty-three

Afterwards, Arcadia travelled through the spirit of poets and composers. Landscapes were idealised in its image. It journeyed through the late Renaissance into the painting of Guercino. He was the first to use the famous inscription, along with a skull, and shepherds surprised in their confrontation with death in Arcadia. But in Guercino the inscription is not central. The emphasis is on the nature of their surprise.

And the Arcadian ideal finds its perfect resting or haunting place in Poussin, who executed the painting twice before he found its most perfect form.

The idea of the inscription in Poussin's painting had its true origins in Virgil, in the fifth eclogue, called *Daphnis at Heaven's Gate*, in which two shepherds come upon the tomb of Daphnis and sing of his deification. For Daphnis existed in the Theocritus original, but was raised even higher by Virgil. In the *Eclogues*, Daphnis is a great and original poet, and Virgil is lamenting the death of a beloved contemporary. Daphnis was famous, gifted, and beautiful and he died young. In the poem Virgil lifts him up to Heaven, to become a minor star, a little deity.

And so in literary terms it was Daphnis, the poet, who was saying: 'I too have lived in Arcadia'. It is the inscription you might find on the tomb of a famous poet, a genius, which seems to say: 'I, with consciousness heightened to life's innumerable beauties, sufferings, and marvels; I, a celebrant of life's mysteries; I, in whom the wonder of all things was richly alive in love and in art; I too was once like you, happy, unhappy, alive, and in love. I too was wild and young and loved. And now I'm dead. But remember: I too lived the happiness of Arcadia.'

Twenty-four

But in the alchemy of Poussin's painting, something even more mysterious and haunting takes place.

The inscription stands alone.

The removal of a name makes it ambiguous.

The tomb could be Everyman, could be any one of us.

Or it could be no one.

It could just be the house of Death, the fact of Death, the reality of Death.

But it hints also that it is only here, in Arcadia, in mortality, in life, on earth, that Death has its home, its dominion.

In Virgil the dead poet transcends death by being lifted up to Heaven's Gate. In Virgil, therefore, we can all be received at Heaven's Gate.

There is transcendence in Virgil, the poet.

There is no hint of transcendence in Poussin.

There is just the bare statement of fact, an impenetrable fact: 'I too lived in Arcadia'.

This fact is a labyrinth without any exit. It is closed.

The mind either learns to live within the closed labyrinth of the conjoining of death and life;

Or the mind develops wings, and soars.

Before the interview began, Lao made a pact with his spirit, with his mind.

That he would be among those who learn to live within the labyrinth, that he would join those who develop wings and soar.

Twenty-five

Dialogue in a Labyrinth

The director of the museum wore a red scarf over his shoulder and a dark suit. The red scarf seemed to energise him. He spoke with great enthusiasm and feeling. Like all experts, he was not interested in dialogue, only in communicating what he had contemplated for many years. At first this absence of dialogue was irritating to Lao, who saw the film as a quest, not as a lecture, as dance, not as monument. But Lao made concessions, and much that was fruitful emerged from the clanking of their armour.

Lao: It is a pleasure to meet you, Director, and a pleasure to be here at the Louvre, in the presence of the genius of Poussin. Our film is about Arcadia and its incarnation in art, music, literature, and the human spirit. You are an expert on the work of Nicolas Poussin. Can you tell us something about this painting and Arcadia and what it whispers to us about human life?

Director: Absolutely. It is a very famous picture. It is an icon of classicism. And it tells us a sad story, in a way. The story is simple: there are four people, they are walking into a landscape, and they discover a tomb. On this tomb is written Et in Arcadia Ego. They are looking at this inscription. They are in various stages of understanding. One of them is showing the inscription to a girl, a beautiful girl. But what does the inscription mean? It means that even in Arcadia, even in earthly paradise, even where everyone is happy, death is present. These four are discovering the existence of death. Two of them are looking very happy together, but now they know that this happiness will end...

Lao: How do you account for its fame?

Director: It's hard to say. It was originally commissioned by a cardinal and he wanted a quality of moral poetry in the painting.

Lao: A beautiful phrase – moral poetry.

Director: The painting is a meditation, and something more. That is always Poussin's greatness. He is not only a man of events. He is also a man of thinking, of thought.

Lao: In Guercino's painting there is a skull.

Director: Yes, and also in the first version of Poussin's painting. But in this second version the skull has disappeared. It has now become not even a dead man, but Death.

Lao: Tell me about this quality of contemplation.

Director: Well, there is also the fact that we find ourselves looking at the picture. We are enjoying it. But we know at the same time that one day we will no more enjoy the picture.

Lao: So the painting should induce a sense of humility, and also a sense of enjoying what is present because the present is the only thing that is real. This is why I am fascinated by the painting. It poses – or rather it brings together this complementary relationship between death and happiness. The inevitability of death and also the possibility of happiness. Is one to take from this painting the feeling that a wise sense of death should increase our capacity for happiness because we realise how transient life is? Or should it make us sober, humble, reflective, quieter, less ambitious?

Director: These are the questions that Poussin would have liked you to ask. In a way, Poussin doesn't give answers to such questions. He prefers you to find yourself asking such questions in front of his pictures. But he leaves you free to choose what you like. Especially at this point in his career. He is still a young man.

Lao: How old would you say?

Director: Between thirty-eight and thirty-nine.

Lao: Why has this picture caught the imagination of the world?

Director: To my mind it is not the greatest picture of Poussin. But to answer your question I think that it was a very clear image of death for the succeeding centuries. Its artistry and iconography have been much studied and many have tried to explain this special painting.

Lao: But why does happiness, Arcadia, and a sense of tranquillity have to be opposed with death in order for us to feel them more strongly?

Director: For centuries many have discussed the meaning of the inscription. Some say that Poussin made a mistake in his interpretation of the Latin words. Perhaps chance has entered into its enigma.

(Lao laughed. The director continued.)

Director: But also painters use images, not words. They don't need to be precise with words. Poussin makes us concerned and involved with what is going on in the painting. The cardinal told Poussin to paint 'Et in Arcadia Ego'; and he had to transform this brief into an image. He seems to want it interpreted in different ways. You spoke about ambiguity. I think that in a way if you close the image, if you have all the answers to your question about a picture...

Lao: Oh, it dies, it dies...

Director: Yes, it dies. And being a diligent painter he knew that by not giving a clear answer to this question he would maintain the attention and the intentions of the centuries towards his works of art. He knew that death is there and that we all die; but he also knew that this picture tells us something about himself and that creating these images is his way of surviving.

Lao: I'd like to ask you a private question about the Arcadian theme. One cannot say with any certainty that everyone has an Arcadia. But one can say that everyone needs an Arcadia. Listening to you speak with such feeling about Poussin's painting makes me wonder whether you too have some private place of enchantment. What is your Arcadia?

Director: Well, I think it is the Louvre on a Tuesday, a day when the museum is closed and the museum is all my own. I also think that in a certain way museums are the Arcadias of our age.

Lao: Tell me more about that.

Director: When you see the crowds in the museum on certain days you find yourself wondering about this, about Arcadia. But when the museum is nearly empty people come in here and I'm quite sure they find their Arcadia here.

Lao: What form does it take?

Director: Meditation. Walking round the museum. Enjoying an image. Singing to one's self. Going backwards and forward. Being able to escape from everyday life, from the rumours of the city. I'm quite convinced that the great success of museums in our day, and not just the Louvre, is in part connected with Arcadia. Evasion might also be a good word.

Lao: There is in Arcadia the notion of escape, but also that of death.

Director: Yes.

Lao: Does the painting suggest that a sense of death and its inevitability might increase one's sense of peace?

Director: Many people think that museums are the churches of our age. In churches you had to learn how to face death. Some pictures teach us how to face death with dignity and with greatness. Poussin was a stoic. There is beauty in facing things the right way.

Lao: What is this stoic attitude to beauty. Is it because Arcadia and beauty are linked?

Director: For Poussin the purpose of art was delectation. The moral lesson of the picture is crucial, but at the end the real point of his pictures was delectation and pleasure. He did not try to please the crowds. He was more inclined to do pictures for the happy few.

Lao: One final question. Could you elaborate on the idea that the museums of this world also constitute an Arcadia?

Director: People come here to forget the troubles of everyday life. They come here because they know that contact with great masterpieces improves them in a way. There is in museums a morality. There is a way of life. In our age one feels that those in charge of museums have to think deeply on such points and about the public's continual coming here. The public do not only expect to see great works of art. They expect something more, and we have to try to find out what it is exactly. Arcadia is a good answer.

Twenty-six

And then there was the swift departure from the labyrinth of the Arcadian painting. The swift departure from the centre. To catch the train to Switzerland. The city was boiling. Paris was nervy. People were whirling in and out of their daily problems. The crowded streets. The struggle to earn a living. The stress of maintaining a persona, a style, an identity, an inner structure. The cracks in the masks. The anxiety bleeding out in nervous glances. The persistence of poverty. The chaos undermining confidence in the future. Uncertainty stalking every individual. And underneath it all a strain, a refrain of something in the inscription. For the whole crew had been infected by it; and Lao now saw it everywhere.

On the way to the Gare de l'Est, Lao passed a beggar. At the station there was the crowding and the crush, and the insistent refrain. There were the faces. The sense of loss, of disorientation. Eyes trapped in the spell of distraction. Everyone trying to get somewhere, to continue their journeys. Where was everyone trying to go? What was the insistent refrain that had haunted the journey from the very beginning?

Then Lao saw it, briefly. He saw a man with thick glasses, struggling to make out the words on the giant console. Struggling to make out his destination, to see it clearly. He was adjusting his glasses, straining, sweating, and still he couldn't see clearly.

Twenty-seven

Anxiety and stress. Bewilderment and stress. Is it death that secretly troubles us? Are we too, like the shepherds, trying to decipher the inscription?

BOOK SEVEN

One

Is it that we don't feel entirely at home in the world? Or is it that the world we have made doesn't quite correspond to the dreams and hopes that somewhere dwell in us?

Lao looked out of the window of the train as it sped on to Switzerland. His thoughts troubled him. The world is not as we would have liked it. Lao surveyed the panorama of the earth, serene within his anxieties. He looked out on the fields and churches, the clusters of houses. And as the scenes shot past him so did his thoughts. He thought of the world as we have made it. Wars across nations. Refugees across borders. Walking without hope or food towards hostile destinations. With all their meagre possessions on their heads. In the tribal battles of the world. Families dying of starvation. Dying from famine. In camps. Dying under the sun. Devoured by flies. Breathing the poisoned air of corrupt and wicked governments. Dying under the filmed gaze of the world. Environmental disasters everywhere. Pollution everywhere. Wars of religion. Wars of race. Wars of creed. Wars of economics. Wars of fear. Wars of ideology. Wars all over the world.

The homeless all across the globe. Tribal peoples deprived of their land. Invisible imperialisms spreading their cancer all over the earth. Diseases ravaging unloved millions. Poverty multiplying like bacilli. Oceans drained of their fishes. Animals rare and free perishing all across the plains. Toxic wastes in the water and air and food. Nuclear bombs hanging over our destinies. Human freedoms eroded by giant powers. Injustices and inequalities raging across the globe, but concentrated in the vast continents that are also the poorest and the most exploited. The people who live on minimal hope, in shanty towns, in squatter camps, living side by side with overspilling latrines.

Is this the world we dreamed of before birth? Is this the world that childhood promised in its golden glories of innocence?

Two

Lao was troubled. Even in countries where there is no mass hunger, there is anomie. Mass silent despair. Even amidst plenitude and excess. Lives lived with no sense of purpose. From school to university then to the workplace. Working to earn a living, then to pay the mortgage, then to raise children. Then what? Where does it all lead? What is the purpose of all that energy, all that fire, all that effort, all that love, all that rage, all that chaos, all that dreaming?

Emptiness and absence of religion. Humiliation and no sense of redemption. Just work and television and sex and entertainment. Loves that fail. Marriages that die. Hopes that perish with the onset of adulthood. Knowledge that drives away the freshness of innocent dreaming. The joy of freedom that shrinks into the fear of being. Cynicism and despair. The fear of old age and the fear of dying. The perplexity of youth. The fear of losing one's youth. The terror of accumulating wrinkles. The decaying of the teeth. The falling out of the hair. The inevitable decline. The thickening of the waistline, the bloating of the belly, the loss of youth's vigour and freshness. The endless battles in the marketplace, the offices, the corporations, the rat race. The endless repetition of waking up in the morning, going to work, coming back, sleeping, waking up again, on and on, with no destination to make sense of it all, nothing that adds up to some redeeming whole, or goal.

A life is seldom a work of art. There is no sense of achievement in having made it, of having shaped it, or of it having a meaning and a value beyond itself, a value to others, something that shines beyond mortality.

Why go on living? How often does living seem like a finely drawn out ritual of humiliation and meaninglessness? All our intelligence, all our achievements, all our efforts, our schemes and plans, our designs, all that obeying of the laws and dictates of society, all that compromise between our secret selves and public selves, where does it all lead, what monument does it crystallise, into what light does it resolve? Why does there have to be emptiness after so much presence in the world? Why does it all have to end in a grave with an inscription which, more or less, says: 'I too have loved, suffered, and been wretched, been successful and neurotic, been confused and despairing, in Arcadia'?

Three

On all the faces Lao looked upon in the train, he saw traces of disaster, of mortality's terrors, the ironies of time. Faces that were giving off quiet concealed despair. Faces cracking and leaking, lights that are dying. Faces that carried their secret troubles with them across the speeding landscape.

Lao was troubled by the troubles in people's faces, in their souls. The train soon seemed to him to be a symbol of something mysterious, bearing people to unknown destinations that were not really destinations, places that were the antechambers of dying, not the beginning of living. He saw trains suddenly as capsules of despair mixed with dreams, escape pods in which the seeds of destiny travelled in the souls of the travellers. They carried their fates with them like flowers pollinated with dying and living, with good and evil, with disaster and illumination. What a mixed heritage is humanity on a train speeding to the spilling place where lives pour out towards their ambiguous destination.

Did we dream the world thus? Or do we project the wrong dreams upon the world, and thereby make it our nightmare? Is the nightmare of reality within or is it without? Where will the healing begin? Lao wondered. Can the world be remade from without? Can the cracked walls of reality be fixed from the outside? Can the starving people be fed only from without, and can feeding them solve the problems that brought them to the point of starvation in the first place?

Where is the world first made, within or without? And where must the world first be remade? Must we first remake the world within, remake our minds, our hearts, our thoughts? Or must we first, like builders without a design, without a plan, remake the world, improve the world, brick by brick, with no sense of the overall picture?

Four

Where did the betrayal start? Lao thought. Where did the discrepancy begin? Was the world broken, its arches collapsed, its columns fallen, its bridges in ruins, before we were born, before we tumbled forth onto the wrecked stage of humanity?

Where must the healing begin – this question thundered in Lao's mind to the relentless rhythm of the train as it ground its way over iron, sparking fire, towards its ceasing point in Switzerland.

Where must the healing begin? Have we lost faith in our capacity to dream things better, and make the world shape itself in accordance with this better and juster dreaming? Have we lost the will to live without the ringing humiliation that so encircles our lives in other people's suffering? Can we still find a way to make the world correspond to our best dreams and hopes?

Where must the healing begin? Do we make the world we see? Do we project onto the world the despair that we feel, the terror that we sense, the hopelessness that sometimes overwhelms us? Lao thought hard about this.

There is no despair or terror or hopelessness in the sky, the flowers, the bees, the horses, the cats, the wind, the sea, or the mountains. If they perish it is because of time, or the atmospheric conditions we have helped create, or nature's own upheavals. But despair does not cling to the air as a flea does to succulent living flesh. Terror does not reside in the sky. Hopelessness does not fall with the autumn leaves. These things are in our minds. They are in us. They dwell in us, and we have given them a habitation, a home. They stare out at the world from within the fabric of our own seeing.

So the cosmic illness, the anomie, the despair, the terror, the nausea, the emptiness, are all within. We are the sickness. We harbour our own malaise, and then we project it onto the world. And then we sink into apathy and hopelessness, into self-centredness, and self-protectiveness. We stop seeing. We no longer notice the signs that are sent us. We no longer notice the messages sent us, intended to wake us up, to remind us of who we are, to guide us to the moment of initiation into our true kingdom. We become the totality of our disease. We become the condition that we harbour, that we project, that we blame on the world.

And then we stop seeing the world. The world becomes an enemy. People become vague antagonists. Then the world mirrors what we have put into it in our diseased seeing. The disease is within. The world is more or less neutral, but the disease within makes it seem an enemy, corrupt, fallen from grace, hopelessly irredeemable, impossibly unhealable. Then, with these perceptions, it becomes possible to live as if living were dying, when living is really living, open-ended, till death. And maybe even beyond.

With these perceptions, we separate ourselves from nature and from others. We become double exiles from the universe and from humanity, from love and from life, from the past and the present, from history and from the future. We are not even at home in here, now, in our bodies, in time, in our dreams. We wander through time, with no destination in sight. And so, inadvertently, we make death our homecoming, with the grave as our home.

But the grave is home only to the bones. Not to the spirit. It is not a home to the spirit.

Five

And as he looked at each member of the scattered crew, all concealing the brink of their nervous breakdowns, and as he pondered the ghosts of failures and fears that they all carried with them on the journey, Lao thought about the messages.

He thought about the signs, and the inscriptions everywhere that become clear only when we see them. And like a thread in a labyrinth, they lead out to the open universe, where intuitions sparkle in the night sky of the mind. Our redemption is always there, here, waiting, in the air we breathe, in our heartbeats, in our thoughts. We only have to want it and the healing, quietly, begins. Home is here, in time, and in timelessness. Exile ends when we sense that home is everywhere that the soul can sing from. The messages have no greater power than the terror to bring the news of our awakening.

Where must the healing begin, the train thundered at Lao as he stared at his fellow passengers as they sat reading their books, their newspapers, staring out of the windows not into the passing landscape but into passing memories fears hopes dreams regrets sadnesses and losses.

Maybe the healing must begin within, thought Lao.

Six

Is it death that secretly troubles us?

Mistletoe paused in her drawing to contemplate the thought that had suddenly drifted into her mind from the swirling anxieties of her fellow passengers.

Where had the thought come from?

Mistletoe was one of nature's non-worriers. She was blessed with the gift of travelling through time and life's disasters with a serenity that astonished those who knew her. She had no philosophy as such. She had no worked-out ideology. And she had none of the overwhelming ambitions that drove people on frantically down life's narrow roads. She viewed life as a journey, and harboured no thoughts about its end. The journey was all that ever concerned her.

She was born with a happy soul. She had made as many mistakes as most people make in an average life in any of the privileged nations of the earth. Her parents were both still alive and so, without knowing it, she was still dwelling in enchanted time, without the invisible and searing umbilical cord ever having been cut. She was in the blessed zone of her life, and didn't know it. Still – she had, with tranquillity, been making experimental drawings of the merging scenes that fast travel makes of the world, when the question materialised in her mind. Her drawing was troubled by the question.

Is it death that secretly troubles us? The fear that the marvel of being alive will be no more? That we will no longer breathe, or see the buttercups of May? That we will love no more, no more be loved? That all the sweet things we take so much for granted will be extinguished: the pleasures of reading, the delight of travel, the ecstasies of lovemaking, all the wonderful surprises that life might bring, that all will be as the promise of summer glimpsed in winter, but not lived to be seen? This troubled her.

When all the possibilities of life, when all the failures of a life so far, when all the despair, the fears, the worries, are set against death, how feeble all our fears, worries, and failures seem. The fear of death narrows the perspective of life, narrows it, and makes all of living shrink.

The fear of death makes life not worth living. It makes life a sort of living death. For it gives death such power and such hegemony over every act of living. Fear of death makes death into a tyrant that commands all the laws and routes of living. It makes life surrender to death, to a future death, to a thing that has not yet occurred, and so it abolishes the entire scope and freedom of living while one is alive.

Seven

Mistletoe wasn't thinking any more. Like Lao, she was listening to thoughts from the open universe. Thoughts that were there, in the air, responding to the intensity of questions sent out from the beseeching heart into the vital spaces.

One moment she was on the train hurtlingly bound for Switzerland. The next she was nowhere, or was it everywhere, so deep in thought-listening was she. Lao was there in everywhere. And the crew were all there too. And all the passengers on the train. And all travellers on all journeys. And all people all over the world. And yet it felt as if she were there alone, breathing in intuitions that lit up in her as she paused between art and thoughts on the fear of death.

What was she listening to?

Not words, not songs, not forms, not sounds, not ideas, not philosophies, not answers, not solutions. Just energies. Energies that she let percolate or collect or crystallise or dance in her mind and pass away not even leaving behind a shadow, but maybe a fragrance of distilled eternity. And every now and again she would catch a look from Lao, and the look would be a thought that she would hear and mix in with the distilled moments.

Eight

Intuitions on the Way (1)

Is it death that secretly troubles us? she asked again, as she listened to the higher silence beyond the speeding train. And then she heard it again. Live while you are alive.

While alive, life ought to be the dominant principle, the master force, the motive power. How much more is possible when one chooses life over death, freedom over fear, love over hate. All the great possibilities unexplored in history and the thousand biographies of the great ones are but the beginning and the foundation of amazing new ways of living, of working and dreaming one's way out of the corner we find ourselves in if we but choose life over death, hope over fear, a greater self-image over a smaller one.

Then living expands and becomes a wonderful chess game. A magic playground. A mischievous game of sublime poker.

Invisible ones watch to see how we play the game with the deceptive cards we have been dealt.

The game lies not in the cards, but in the players.

There is also the projection of value and power into things.

It is not about winning. The game continues beyond time. The genius of openness.

Mastery is the key to mystery.

Time is a factor.

There are more factors than are apparent.

Life is living. The surprising ways of continuing to be alive.

There is freedom. Freedom in the spirit of playing.

Connect infinite intelligence.

Life is as open or as closed as you care for it to be. As you love it enough to be. As you dare...

Life is your thing. Your game. Your joke. Play it and love it as you will.

All great things have a quality of humour in them. The sheer cheek.

All great things smile at the economy of vision. Seeing so much in so little.

The humility. The miracle.

The humour is in the seeing. The wonderful risk.

Ought to have reverence for the powers that reside within, waiting to be used for nothing, or for immortal marvels.

Nine

Intuitions on the Way (2)

Mistletoe often remembers a favourite story of Lao's. It came to her now. The story goes like this. You die, and find yourself, like Daphnis, at Heaven's Gate. A mysterious person meets you at the entrance. You ask to be admitted. The mysterious person insists first on a conversation about the life you have lived. You complain that you had no breaks, that things didn't work out for you, that you weren't helped, that people brought you down, blocked your way, that your father didn't love you, that your mother didn't care, that economic times were bad, that you didn't have the right qualifications, that you didn't belong to the right circle, that you weren't lucky, in short you pour out a veritable torrent of excuses. But for every excuse you bring forth the infinitely patient mysterious person points to little things here and there that you could have done, little mental adjustments you could have made. He gently offers you examples of where, instead of giving up, you could have been more patient. Tenderly, he shows you all the little things you could have done, within the range of your ability, your will, that would have made a difference. And as he offers these alternatives you see how perfectly they make sense, how perfectly possible the solutions were, how manageable. You see how, by being more alive to your life, and not panicky and afraid, things could have been so much more livable, indeed, quite wonderful.

You suddenly see that you could have been perfectly happy during all the time that you were perfectly miserable. That you could have been free instead of being a prisoner. That you could have been one of the radiant ones of the earth. That living could have been fun. It could have been worthwhile. That life could have been a playground of possibilities. It could have been a laboratory of intelligence and freedom. And living could have been composed of experiments in surprise, in immortality. Experiments in the art of astonishment. Fascinating time-games. Space-games. Dimension-games.

You suddenly see that living is the place where gods play within mortal flesh. An open-ended play in which dying is the most open-ended ending of them all, opening out into the infinity of nothingness, or into the infinity of absolute being.

Therefore, living is the place of secular miracles. It is where amazing things can be done in consciousness and in history. Living ought to be the unfolding masterpiece of the loving spirit. And dying ought to set this masterpiece free. Set it free to enrich the world. A good life is the masterwork of the magic intelligence that dwells in us. Faced with the enormity of this thought, of the Damascene perception, failure, despair, unhappiness, seemed a small thing, a gross missing of the point of it all.

Ten

'Is it death that secretly troubles us?' said Mistletoe aloud, quite suddenly, without knowing why.

'I was asking myself the same question,' said Lao.

They were both silent for a while. Alive in time and timelessness. The train bore them towards Arcadia.

'Is it death that secretly troubles you?' asked Lao, eventually.

'No,' replied Mistletoe.

Then, dreamily, she added:

'It's life that ought to fascinate us.'

'And make us hungry for more life.'

'More joy.'

'More fun.'

'More love.'

'More laughter.'

'More freedom,' said Mistletoe, daughter of Pan.

'More justice,' said Lao, the mental outlaw.

'More light,' said both of them, in chorus, laughing gently.

Then they fell silent again, and stared wistfully out of the window of the train. To a world looking in, they could be inscriptions.

London
September 2001

A letter from the publisher

We hope you enjoyed this book. We are an independent
publisher dedicated to discovering brilliant books,
new authors and great storytelling. Please join us at
www.headofzeus.com and become part of our
community of book-lovers.

We will keep you up to date with our latest books, author
blogs, special previews, tempting offers, chances to win
signed editions and much more.

If you have any questions, feedback or just want to say hi,
please drop us a line on hello@headofzeus.com

 @HoZ_Books

 HeadofZeusBooks

www.headofzeus.com

The story starts here